POOL OF SOULS
AND OTHER STORIES

by

DANIEL JOHN KLEIN

First Printing, 1996; Second Printing, 2000;
Third Printing, August 2004;
Fourth Printing, November 2015
© 2024 Daniel John Klein
Registered with WGAw

Cover and text design by
Daniel J Klein

published by

Interactive

M E D I A

E-mail: daniel@lightinteractivemedia.com

ACKNOWLEDGMENTS

This is the fifth printing of *Pool of Souls*. It's had a helping hand from new writing mentors to get some attention for a big run at self-publishing. I could get naked in the middle of the street and that would get attention, but it's already been done before. Not by me.

This time around, I had the great help of Eleanor Harder, Professor of English at UCLA, who was tough on me, but fair in her insightful and right-on-the-money take on the stories. Most of all, I want to thank my screenwriting mentor, the late Ken Rotcop, who taught me to stay on the spine of the story and who browbeat me into writing when I didn't want to. He had a gift, no doubt about it and I miss him terribly. Thank you all.

Thanks always to Betti and Adrian for guiding me to a personal relationship with God through Jesus Christ. And where would I be without God? He deserves all the glory.

And last but first, I thank my wonderful wife, Pannipa, for the laughs that have gotten us through so much and who continues to stretch my vocabulary with her ESL "Noi-isms". The amazing Thai food she cooks doesn't hurt, either! She's the Apple of my eye…

I hope you enjoy the stories as much as I do. Who wrote these things, anyway?

WHEN I
WORKED FOR THE CIRCUS

My brother said it was at the park, in Pewaukee, but I know it was at the place that used to be the landfill. We referred to it as "the dump". It was right next to the park. And it didn't rain that whole three days the circus was in town. Good thing, too, because the ground at the old landfill was just dirt and gravel. Everything would have sunk into the muck and barely covered up garbage and it wouldn't have brought anyone out there – even me.

That first day of summer vacation was clear and hot, no haze. Any kind of activity produced a good, clean sweat. It was the end of the first week of my summer vacation. I was fifteen on the road to sixteen and, fortunately for me, I had already begun the slowing down towards adulthood, reaching a cruising speed I like to think I still maintain today.

In an orange T-shirt with a pocket, and green Levi's, I was pedaling slowly down the straight and flat park road, my stingray bike perched in what I planned to be the longest wheelie ever attempted. Just the year before, I had sold my big green paper route bike to another paperboy to get this little, three-speed stick-shift model. My best friend, Kurt, gave me a good deal on the bike so I bought it, knowing that soon I would have to get rid of the bike and start hitchhiking as a prelude to getting my driver's license.

Kurt sold it to me cheap, I think because he had acquired new respect for me when I finally defended myself after he hit me in the stomach with a big two-by-four. Before that time, he used to do things like that on a regular basis to see how much he could get away with. Being an only child, he usually got away with a lot. Like the time two years earlier when he got me falling-down-drunk on the martinis he made in his mother's supper club bar while she was out for her day-off shopping and we were innocently building model cars in the dining room. It was also while making model cars at age fourteen, a year later, that Kurt talked me into putting my face into a paper bag with airplane cement poured in the bottom for my first real high.

That was when I decided I liked drugs a lot. It was a way for me to get further away, other than just physically, from my dad. Besides, it was much easier to get away with than drinking as evidenced by that martini episode where, after stumbling home from Kurt's — falling down and puking occasionally — I tried to make it up the stairs to the attic bedroom I shared with my two brothers. About halfway up, with my whole family sitting in the living room, all my father says is "Come down here."

I can't imagine what my brothers and sisters and my mom thought as I came back down the stairs to stand there, teetering, white as a grub worm with half-closed eyes and slurred speech, in front of my dad. I suppose they thought at that moment that they didn't know me.

It was one of the few times my dad didn't whack me or otherwise punish me for screwing up. I remember it as the one time he recognized that I had a brain of my own, because he didn't yell at me or anything. He figured I knew all I needed to know about alcohol after a night of warm milk-induced vomiting — thanks to Mom, although she had to clean it all up. I was so sick the next day, I had to stay home from school. The only thing my dad had to say to me when he got home was, "Hit any of the bars today?"

There I was, so entranced in my determination to pull the longest wheelie in Pewaukee's history that I almost didn't see them — two glaring white semi-trucks and an odd assortment of white and off-white trucks, campers, and El Caminos.

Gathered with them around the perimeter of the dump were three other big cattle trucks with all the animals – one just for the elephants – and a few trucks with amusement rides.

The sight was such a surprise that I forgot I had the front wheel up in the air and still pedaling, tried to turn the bike to my left, in the direction of the dump. The bike almost shot out ahead from underneath me and I ended up on the opposite edge of the road, still on the bike, a station wagon full of people laying on the horn as they whizzed by. I was lucky.

But there was a circus! I wondered why there hadn't been any posters or announcements at school. I think it was because they figured all the kids found out something like that in a hurry and then the parents would have no choice.

I didn't realize it then, of course, that in my rapture at finding the circus there at the dump, I didn't even think to go tell any of my friends. The amazing thing was that I completely forgot my reason for going down to the park in the first place. Barbara Garrett was going to be there for activities day. She liked me and I liked her. Well, I hate to admit it, but I really just liked her big breasts. That's all I could think about when I was around her – putting my hands on them – feeling like I was hanging on for dear life.

There was only one thing that could pull my mind away from girls and their body parts – anything totally new and unknown to me.

That's the way I was.

With my head like it was full of iron filings drawn to the magnet of the circus circled wagon train-style around the dump, I wanted only to find out all I could about this circus. Before I knew it, I was pestering one of the guys who seemed like he knew something about how everything worked.

Jack was what he said his name was and I told him right off that my parents said I could work if I wanted, that I was in Boy Scouts, I loved animals, and that I didn't care if I got paid or not, none of which was true. I figured that once they saw how fast and hard I worked and how quickly I caught on, they would pay me anyway, all of which turned out to be true.

After being sized up and inspected by Jack and a couple of the other guys – I hadn't started wearing glasses yet, so that helped – they put me to work. There wasn't anybody else rushing out to get in on the excitement firsthand, so I guess that helped out, too. None of my friends or anybody I knew ever came to work out there. I liked that. I wanted it all to myself. So I could dole out the stories later. I never did tell any stories till now, though, on account of my dad.

When the work got started, I began playing Toby Tyler in my head – a Disney movie about a boy who goes off with the circus and becomes friends with one of the chimpanzees. The very first thing to be done was to put up the tent.

What better advertisement than seeing a huge red and white tent at the dump while on your way to the park! And get this – they really used the elephants to raise the center poles on the tent. It was just like they did in the movie. Some of the bigger ropes they used were about as big around as a super fat bratwurst and just as greasy. The elephant near us had one of the big ropes in some kind of harness around its neck and they backed him up, raising the pole that was wedged into a hole so the bottom couldn't go anywhere and so the top pulled right up. I didn't ask about it, but I figured that they made the elephants go backward instead of forward so the elephant didn't decide to take off running, carrying the tent with it out of the dump.

It didn't seem as if the elephants had to work very hard to raise those poles, but they were watered down and fed after they were done just the same. I thought that was a nice way to treat them.

Our job was next and we had to put up all the poles around the outside of the tent and stake them into the ground. There were some younger guys who lived with their parents in the circus and worked with me putting up poles. It was tough work and they noticed that I wasn't able to do as much as them, but they were friendly to me and kidded me about coming with them to the next town if I built up some muscles in the next few days. One of the guys let me have a pair of old gloves to protect me from rope burns and splinters but I didn't catch his name. I was too consumed with all of this new stuff to think to ask names and such. All in all, there wasn't a great amount of conversation with anyone while we worked. It was just too hot. And there was too much to do to get ready.

Jack "hustled us up a little" so we could get to putting up the bleacher-like stands for the audience in the tent. It was like a blast furnace in the tent, but I enjoyed setting up the seating because it was so systematic and organized. And you had to think a little bit to get the right sections of bleacher in the right place. I had to correct the guys a couple of times and I thought this was strange because they had done this so many times and this was my first.

At almost five o'clock we finished with the seating, which was good because I needed to go home for supper, and boy-oh-boy, was I beat! I was so tired and worn out that I thought I was going to throw up. I felt good inside, though, from doing good work and being appreciated for it.

Jack asked when I would be back that evening and I had to tell him that it might be about six-thirty or maybe not until in the morning – just in case Dad wouldn't let me come back at all. He said it was okay if it was early in the morning and that it might be better. I think he knew I was going to need that night off to rest up from the afternoon. I was glad, because *I* knew I needed the rest, but didn't want to let on that fact – not to any of the circus people or to my parents.

Mom liked to think I was different because I was the only one of my five brothers and sisters who took after her side of the family. I did seem to be sick more often than the others and my hair is now falling back south to Nashville, where mom's bald-headed family is from, but I think I was just allergic to my dad.

He wouldn't be home from the factory in Milwaukee until five-thirty so there was plenty of time to work on my mother. She got home about four-fifteen after working at the laun-dro-mat.

After school, I sometimes would go down and help her out with things so she could get out of there a little early. I did things like putting extra single-use boxes of detergent and bleach in the coin-vended machines. Filling the Coke machine was fun because I got to see the inside of it and could continue trying to figure out how to get free cokes out of it if you didn't have the key. Mom would always let me take a cold one out while I was filling it up.

After I struggled to pedal back up the park road, it didn't take too long to prep Mom for the battle with Dad. She could tell that I was really happy with what I had done that day and since I hadn't been happy all that much for the last couple of years, she was quick to say yes and added that she would fix him his southern favorite – pan-fried chicken.

Now came the really tough part. I hated asking my dad for anything. If he didn't say no, which was most of the time, he usually gave me a hard time about it being a stupid thing to do or rhetorically asking, "Why would you want to do something like that?"

To be fair, I suppose there were plenty of times he gave me his consent and even his encouragement. It's just that his refusals were so intimidating and my requests for reasons why I couldn't do something brought on such quick anger in him, it made me fear his response to anything.

Near the end of supper and after there had been sufficient conversation about the circus being in town, I decided it was time. Actually, Mom decided it was time ahead of me and she jumped in with, "Danny went down and helped put up the tent today and they're going to let him come back and work the rest of the time it's in town. I told him it was okay if it's okay with you."

The pressure was off! Now I just had to bear his gaze while he contemplated this brazen act of initiative. First of my mother's and then of mine. Although he never called *her* a brainless idiot, the way he looked at her sometimes indicated the same. This time, he let us both off the hook. He wouldn't let me go back that evening, but I could go back for the next two days that the circus was in town. After all, letting me go back that night was being just too lenient – on both me *and* my mom.

The next morning I woke up early, bathed, and put on my favorite stretch Levi's and a real conservative plaid short-sleeved shirt and rode back down to the dump.

The night before, the circus people had put up all the concession stands, the few rides and games, lights, and the big Funhouse – which was the only thing that I was going to miss out on while working that I really cared about. Anyway, I could always tell how the games were all rigged so it was next to impossible to win anything and most of the rides just went around in circles and made me sick. The Funhouse was good because you could have a few laughs but mostly because you could try and get girls in there to feel them up there in the dark sections without them knowing for sure who did what. The girls didn't mind it either because a guy couldn't tell just whose tits he was grabbing unless it was a fat girl or another guy.

Speaking of fat girls, it was the fat lady who I was to work with all that morning and the next, getting all the bags of peanuts and popcorn filled and ready for the performances. When Jack introduced us, he seemed very reverential towards the fat lady. Her name was Evon and although she seemed very nice and had a sweet voice, my aversion to fat people kept me from giving her much consideration at all.

First, we bagged up all the peanuts for the afternoon and evening shows. The peanuts came in two sizes – small and large – and after they were all filled, we rolled the tops down and stapled them shut.

This was so I could throw them without them spilling out on everyone.

I was going to be the Peanut Man for the evening performances. The circus had a contract with the Planters Company that gave them a big discount for advertising that they sold Planters peanuts. In Pewaukee, the advertising was going to be me. I had to wear a big peanut body and a black cardboard top hat – just like Mr. Peanut. The only reason I consented to this was because the top hat would cover my entire head with the brim resting on the top of the peanut at neck level, and eyeholes cut out in the middle to see through.

Nobody would know it was me. And I couldn't say no if I wanted to stay around working. For the afternoon performances, I just wore my regular clothes and a white apron and service hat.

All the time the fat lady and I were filling those white bags with hot, freshly popped popcorn and roasted peanuts, I noticed that she didn't eat even one single kernel or peanut. How could she be that fat if she didn't eat stuff like that? She must have weighed four hundred pounds, easy. I would inhale a handful with every bag I filled – and I was skinny.

Though I didn't look much at the fat lady, I asked her every question I could about the circus. She answered every one of them. And right, too, because I threw in a couple of trick questions to see if she wasn't just making things up. Questions like, what's another name for an elephant that begins with a "p". I knew that one from the Toby Tyler movie. It's what the huckster called them when he was out in front of the tent trying to get people to go in.

"COME SEE THE PACK-EE-DERMS, DI-RECT FROM DISTANT INDIA, PRANCING AND PERFORMING PERILOUS FEATS IN A PAGEANT PAR EXCELLENCE!" or something like that. She knew that one, also, and proceeded to tell me about how pachys was Greek for thick and derma was skin.

Gosh, to find an adult that would answer all my questions! I was in heaven. Plenty of times I found adults who gave me wrong answers. Another thing I noticed about Evon was that she didn't sweat one drop standing there in front of that hot popcorn machine on that hot day at the dump in Pewaukee. I think if my dad would have answered my questions at all, he would have been right every time, just like Evon.

I got to see a lot of the performance that afternoon there in the tent, while yelling "PEANUTS!" and expertly tossing the little white bags of pre-warmed peanuts into outstretched hands. People seemed to like to buy them from me – I gave them a smile for their change and wiggled my ears for their kids.

There were, of course, some of my friends at the performance that afternoon, but they didn't give me too hard a time. I think because I was really good at what I was doing but mostly because the circus, for its small size, was excellent. In big circuses, there are multiples of everything, from acrobats to lions. At our circus, there was just about one of everything. Not including the trapeze artists and clowns.

And the pachyderms.

When my duties following that Saturday afternoon show were done, I rushed home for an uneventful and non-confrontational dinner. I had too much stuff in my head to give my dad much trouble. One thing about me is that when I do something, I *become* that thing.

And Saturday night, I became Mr. Peanut. Right down to the jaunty step and crooked elbows. Jack found me a cane to hang over one arm and some white gloves and I was an attraction all by myself. Never in a million years would I have done it if anyone knew it was me.

My family knew. And it turned out that they all showed up for the performance that night. I saw them near the far corner of the tent and Mom spotted me right off and pointed, saying something to

Dad. He looked over my way with squinting eyes and sort of a smile that looked like it wanted to open up and laugh but things weren't quite funny enough.

Dad liked the circus. I think it attracted him in the same way it did me. The flamboyance; the diversity of activity and personalities; the risk; the independence; and most of all, the nomadic nature of circus life. All of the things he had sacrificed for a family life and a job in the factory were now parading around in front of him. Oddly enough, the fissure that became the crack that became the rupture in my little circus world at age fifteen was started by my mother.

I had avoided working my way over to where my family sat for quite a while but I was caught up in the juggling act and tossing peanuts and ended up close enough for my mom to holler at me, in her laughing and proud southern accent, "HEY DANNY, TH'OW US SOME PEANUTS!". In leaning over as close as the peanut allowed me to lean toward Mom's face to ask her to refrain from any sort of motherly recognition, I spotted Chuck O'Connel sitting directly behind, a shit-eating grin of disbelief across his freckled face.

Already sweating buckets in that peanut suit, it wasn't possible for me to sweat more. I could only hope that Chuck would keep his mouth shut because he was right behind my parents.

I stayed away from them for the rest of the show and got the hell out of there as soon as it ended. There was a back section to the main tent where everything was staged from where I got out of my peanut suit. I stayed in there, yakking with the other workers until I thought my parents would be gone. I was relieved when there was no sign of Chuck, either.

It was about ten o'clock so I hung around and listened to the talk of the circus and amusement workers, and the few girls from town that congregated after the show for a few minutes. The actual performers went to their campers and trailers right after the performance. I felt like I was a part of things and no one made me feel like I wasn't wanted there. On my way around the backside of the tent to urinate off the edge of the landfill, I passed a trailer with some kind of classical music coming from it. I liked to look into people's windows at night, not just for the chance at seeing a girl naked – which I never did – but to see what people did in their lives when no one was watching.

Peeking into the back window where no one outside would see me, what I saw was completely mesmerizing. It was Evon, the fat lady, dancing. *Not just dancing, but ballet dancing.* With all these candles lit and the music and Evon moving so gracefully it all just seemed so incredible to me! It was like the movie scene of silhouettes cast against the tent wall by lanterns. After the garish bright lights and the loud recorded circus music, this scene was hypnotic.

As I was becoming lost to everything else, a hand grabbed me by the shoulder and spun me around to face Jack, who was just then realizing it was me and breaking out into a smile. Jack said "Don't stand out here gawking, come on in for a better look," and pushed me in ahead of him. Evon was surprised to see me and offered me some tea and fancy crackers with some sort of spread on them.

After giving me a hard time about peeking in people's windows, Jack explained that he and Evon were married, and through the course of sixty minutes of conversation, I found out enough about them to smash all of the preconceived notions I'd had about circus people. Jack and Evon told me about how they met at the University and fell in love because they felt they were twins, only with the hots for each other. And about when Evon developed her medical conditions, and how they embarked on a healthy lifestyle except for a Twinkie thing that Jack held onto. Evon fed me some sort of fancy crackers and this pat-tay kind of thing that was real good. And Apple Beer. They asked me about my life, too and what I wanted to do after high school and I told them I didn't really plan to finish, just get my GED and get the heck away. Jack kinda read me the riot act about that and about the value of education and about that time I noticed Evon was getting sleepy or just didn't feel good. She began wheezing and Jack helped her to the back of the trailer after she said good night to me and gave me a kiss on the cheek. That was nice.

While Jack was back there, I looked around at the things in the trailer and found four diplomas on the wall, two for Jack and another two from Marquette University made out to Evon L. Sampling – an undergraduate in Education and a Masters in Educational Psychology. The other two were inscribed to Jack: one, a B.A. in Business from Marquette. The other was a degree in Veterinary Medicine.

There were also photos of them from different times of their life and in a bunch of them, Evon was not anywhere near close to being fat. There was a funny picture of Jack in a red jacket with a bunch of other guys in red jackets and I guess it was a Chamber of Commerce picture or something.

When Jack came out after turning off the light and closing the door quietly, I asked him how Evon was doing. He said that they didn't know how long she would live but that they were doing fine, otherwise. I don't know how it happened, but when he said that, my heart felt so sick I could've cried.

Jack must've noticed because after he made me promise not to tell anyone or act like I knew around Evon, he changed the subject to my schooling again and I asked what good all his and Evon's years at college did for them. This riled him a bit and he began to tell me about how most people view circus people but that Evon used her Education degree to home-school the circus people's kids and that Jack's circus was the only one of its kind running in the black and that it was because of his Business Degree and his ability to care for the animals. That shut me up, boy.

Jack remembered, in a way of letting me know it was time to go, that he had forgotten he meant to take a piss when he found me and that he now had to "pee like a racehorse". I told Jack he was lucky I wasn't pissing when he surprised me but that I had to go now, too. So I went out to urinate, side by side with Jack under the stars at the edge of the landfill.

That night was special. I became an adult, made adult by respectful and open communication.

When I got home, Dad was up, waiting. It was too late, definitely, to be coming home and he was angry. But, after telling me I was riding the thin line of trouble, he asked a few questions – like he was interested – about the other things I did at the circus.

I think that somehow it made him feel good because, when I came out of the bathroom after washing up, he had taken his dentures out and was scrunching his jaws up tight, to look like he had no chin, in a big ear-to-ear grin. It was so hilarious with the way he had pulled a Milwaukee Braves cap way down behind his ears to push them out that I broke out laughing. He laughed too, and then swatted me on the arm, sending me off to bed. Up in the attic room with my brother awake in the bed near mine, he asked me what I had been laughing so hard at. When I told him it was Dad, he couldn't believe it either – that I got away with it all.

I slept a good sleep – no dreams – and was raring to go Sunday morning. Evon and I talked up a storm during our duties that morning. I began noticing things like how clean and manicured her fingernails were and the way she never said "um" when she spoke in that beautiful voice of hers. And although she was extremely obese – make no bones about that – her skin had that porcelain-like quality they talk about in those cosmetic commercials on TV.

Evon invited me to have lunch with her and Jack in their trailer and if I could, I was welcome to meet them after the evening performance for some tea and "social intercourse" – which reminded me I had forgotten all about Barbara and her breasts the whole weekend. We had a "splendid" lunch and as I left to get my peanut box stocked up, Jack divulged that Evon had a little gift for me and that he was going to pay me when I came by that night.

You know, I just felt so good, and so right about myself. It didn't seem like anything could violate so wonderful a feeling.

I was really up for that Sunday afternoon performance. Me in my tight stretch Levi's and my white and green Beach Boys-style button down short sleeve shirt with a box full of still-warm peanuts placed in tight rows ready to toss to anyone who heeded my call for "PEANUTS!"

Only a few minutes into the show, I spotted them. The Girls. And sitting among them was Barbara, prominent in her tight white polo shirt. No problem, I had my peanut moves down so slick, so precise, she couldn't help but be impressed. Or so I thought. Because she was still fuming about me not showing up at the park Friday, two days before. She wouldn't look at me when I came near and between the other girls there was a mix of indignant and merciful stares. But Barbara's anger was not a problem. The real problem – the fate-casting, ego-shattering, and incendiary problem – was that Chuck O'Connel was working his way over to sit with the Girls for an encore performance – not of the circus, but of Dan-Dan-the-Peanut-Man. He wasted no time in informing everyone who mattered, that I had been, would be again that night, Mr. Peanut himself. And it was Chuck who cast the first name. "HEY PEANUT BRAIN!" It was Chuck who called all the names, and my embarrassment-fueled rage grew with each one.

The girls all giggled and when the last name came out, the one after "PEANUT BREATH!", "PEANUT BUTT-ER!" and "PEANUT PAN!", Barbara finally turned around in shock. As that last name permutated from "PEANUT PRICK!" to just plain "PEANUT DICK!", Chuck leaned over and whispered in her ear what I later found out to be something about seeing me in the showers after gym class, and Barbara began laughing uncontrollably at me.

Few things in life get me angry, and even fewer things get me really angry. I was nuts. Don't ever say something that isn't true about me. And I had to keep tossing those goddamned peanuts and making change and smiling because that was my job. But I'd fix old Chuckeroo. I was going to beat the living shit out of him, so I went back over and said to him, glancing at Barbara, "Meet me at your house after the show." That was it. I didn't have to say anything more because how could he back down in front of the girls?

Well, before going home for supper, I went over to Chuck's and promptly bloodied his face in his own front yard. It didn't take more than five minutes to extract an oath to clear things up with Barbara about the size of parts of my anatomy and to never give me trouble again. I was getting used to this fighting business, after giving two black eyes in one week to "friends" who tried to bully and belittle me two months before summer vacation.

I felt bad about hurting Chuck. There is nothing more violent than hitting someone in the face with your fist.

Seeing Dad, jaw set, thumbs hooked into his belt loops, and Mom over at the kitchen sink pretending to clean as I came in to wash up for supper, told me that all of the richness and goodness I had been experiencing in my small life for the last forty-eight hours was about to be ripped from my heart.

Dad always wanted us to admit to whatever transgression he thought we had committed before he lit into us. He needed the justification for his excessive and irrational peaks of anger.

Already trembling, hands at my sides ready to try and protect myself from, if nothing else, the *potentiality* of his anger, we began the routine:

"Where have you been?"

"Nowhere." I say, knowing full well that he sees the grass stains and blood, and that he has already gotten a call about the fight. There's no way I'm going to just stick my head into the guillotine.

"Don't lie to me."

"I'm not."

"Don't lie to me."

"Okay." So I tell him my side of what he already knows, inventing a history of Chuck's viciousness.

"What did I tell you about fighting?"

"But Chuck was messing between me and Barbara… "

"What did I tell you about fighting?"

"What was I supposed to do? What would you… "

"WHAT DID I TELL YOU ABOUT FIGHTING?!"

I was so mad. My brain was beginning to shut down rapidly. I don't think I was breathing. I couldn't speak.

"What are you, some brainless idiot?" he asks, expecting

me to answer "YES! I am."

The brink. I was almost there. Dad had gotten himself there, also. The way he would look halfway away and then back at me with a side glance and frowning and not believing he had offspring the likes of me.

He turned up the voltage.

"You need a haircut. You look like a goddamn hippie."

"I just had one a couple weeks ago," I lied.

He knew it was a lie and he knew how to make me squirm. Three months earlier we had another big argument about my hair and he dragged me down into the basement, ripping my shirt. He made me sit on a stool under a bare light bulb while he used the electric clippers on me with his vice-like fingers gripping my skull. Afterward, I had been free to go up to my room to cry.

"I think you need another one," he says.

"Why can't I have my hair the way I want it?" I ask, definitely going too far. But what's new?

"BECAUSE I SAID SO."

"But why not?" I would love to hear his reasoning sometime, you know?

"I think maybe you should stay home tonight and have your hair cut."

We stride, my dad and I, out past that point where human beings share a common compassion, to stand facing, as only arms and mouths in a grossly kinetic conflict that has no winner at all. It's a point from which he and I will never return together. Only at best, alone.

"I've got to go back down for the last show of the circus, they're going to pay me!" I say.

"YOU'RE NOT GOING TO THAT GODDAMN CIRCUS AND THAT'S IT!"

"*Oh, yes I am going to that goddamn circus!*" I replied, not so loud as he and already crying.

I only remember what happened next as a scene without dialog. If I said something, I'm sure I wasn't aware of it.

Exploding, my father put both hands around my throat, pushing my head upwards, not strangling me, but to hold my head in a rigid position so he could scream in my face. I had no idea what he was saying. I only knew that a man I didn't like had me by the throat and that I had to do anything I could to get away, so I smashed at his forearms with all my strength, breaking his hold on the third blow. He was positively incensed. I pushed out at his chest to put space between us and ran from my father through our living room to the front door. In pushing at the doorknob, it locked, preventing me from opening it before he caught up with me. He grabbed me by the neck again and wrapped his arm around my head in a headlock so tight I heard my jaw pop out of place but couldn't feel it. I hit at him in the ribs and cried until I began to tire and that's when I felt another rhythm through my head against his chest. It was my mother, pounding on Dad's back with her fists and screaming "LET HIM GO!" over and over again.

~~~

The next morning, Monday morning, when there wasn't anyone home to tell me what or what not to do, I rode down to the dump in the rain that had come in the night to see my circus family off. I had entertained thoughts of running away with them, but I was smart enough to know I couldn't get away with it.

They were gone. I had missed them. Jack and Evon and the peanuts and the elephants – pachyderms – and the tents and rides were all gone. Dad had taken them away.

I've since forgiven my father and have come to understanding the method of his love for me. And that understanding has, in turn, shaped my love for him.

But what was left was just the dump, back on that day the rain said goodbye to the circus for me. And in many of the spots where poles had been set and stakes pulled up, the heavy rain was washing away the dirt and gravel, exposing half-decomposed garbage.

It was when I turned around to go home that I saw it, tied with twine around the power pole at the edge of the landfill where Jack and I had christened the night with our urine. It was a small package with bright foil ribbon. I didn't want to open it there in the rain so I walked my bike out through the mud and the garbage and rode home into the garage. Inside the package was fifty dollars in ones and a well-worn paperback copy of Kerouac's <u>On the Road</u>. I turned toward the thrown-open doors, faced upward toward the clearing sky, and lifted the cover to the first page. There was an inscription along with a post office box address written in impeccable handwriting that said,

"TO DANNY, OUR GREAT NEW FRIEND. ON THE ROAD, JACK AND EVON".

I HAVE RHINOCEROS HANDS
The Poem

I have rhinoceros hands

thick, dirt brown.
roaming over you.

pushing and nudging,
abrasive to your soft areas.

I travel fully your plains
and you lay used.

somehow,
you are fulfilled.

POSTCARD

Along this east bank, the river ran more quietly in the late summer. Slender, green reeds waved slowly as clear water swam around their submerged shafts. Sand and small pebbles tumbled with the current along the river bottom in silent motion. Still, the river did have sound to it. A kind of high, percussive tone without rhythm. It synchronized with the sight of the water ever-flowing past the eye, filling one's vision as the sound filled the ear.

The river was not without calm, though. Here and there were small pools, caught by a few good-sized rocks that had been smoothed by the incessant flow of water just over their tops. Smaller rocks served to effectively cut off the flow into the pool. The pools flared like mirrors inside the line of rocks. Yet the pools were also crystal clear. One could see the contents of the pool and at the same time, with the adjustment of focus of the eye, the sky and everything above the level of the pool could be seen.

Reversing the gaze from the image of the sky in the pool and looking up to the sky itself, the gurgling sound of the river magically disappeared. The sky became everything. This summer day the sky was forever overhead. Its blue *blue* the very shell surrounding the Earth. Gigantic, cottony cumulus formations appeared stuck to this field of color.

The clouds, as inactive as they seemed, exerted influence over the land. Shadows presented themselves as the antithesis of the clouds. Where the pure white, lighter-than-air shapes seemed to be completely freed from the confines of the land, the shadows they created darkened the surface. If not for the dancing, waving grass still green from regular rainfall, the shadows might seem oppressive as they changed the colors of all objects in their paths to gray.

But the grass did, indeed, dance. In the now-light-now-dark patchwork of light and shadow, the ebb and flow of movement was like that of a hand brushing across an expanse of fine velvet. And, were it not for this ballet of movement, the breeze that was borne of this hot summer day might not have had the cooling effect that it did. For the breeze wound through the trees nearby and moved over the lawn, bumping the white weathered clapboards, finally making its way in through the window where the man was standing.

The breeze wandered in and about the kitchen past the two glasses of cool lemonade sitting on the cloth of the table. Wet rings formed at their bases and spread. Moisture condensed on the outside of the glasses up to the level of where they had been emptied by slow, deliberate swallows.

Dark patches of color showed on the man's back, behind yellowed suspenders clipped to his light blue cotton pants. He stood on one leg with the other crossed behind, toe tip touching the floor for balance, and one arm up above his shoulder along the inside edge of the window. The light pouring in through the window flowed around him, blurring the outline of his body. It was a warm day and he did not move unnecessarily.

His perspiration mingled with his slightly spicy cologne and mixed with the outdoor air to produce a not unpleasant man's smell. In contrast, the woman's scent was floral combined with the dryness of talcum beneath the dark print wrap that she had been napping in.

Now, as she lay on the bed, her eyes were open, fixed – but not seeing, on the ceiling directly above her. The radio was on, softly playing popular music. The dream she awoke from was just now fading as conscious thoughts began to intrude into her midday quiet. There were no pressing engagements to attend, no relatives to entertain here. It was as it should be – a refuge. And there was ample time to be together, she and he.

He had told her nothing of the previous day's business, content to let there have been none, for that matter. He was considerate in that way, for he never unnecessarily burdened their usually pleasant time together. And she, in turn, spared him her day's minor unpleasantries even though she knew he would not trivialize her daily activities in the way that many men might. Not often was it that a particular situation arose that left signs of dis-ease in her that lasted into the evening.

As she lay there, Lyndan felt very content. Her contentment had a timeless quality that she consciously compared to the cool, easy flow of the breeze through the house or of the water in the river. It also felt as though it were unending, that it would not suddenly dry up and leave her with the life that her sisters lived. *That* she could not bear.

Her sisters, both having married and staying in their hometown, lived the life that was the norm for the human race at this time – relative material affluence and spiritual/emotional bankruptcy. They were not, nor would they ever likely to be content with their lives. The two, each one in a different way, strove to gain personal fulfillment from the outside world. Other people, other jobs, other possessions – that is what would make them happy or sad; they just knew it.

And they did their best to get Lyndie to join them in their struggle. But her fulfillment was complete and could not be undone. She had worked very hard for it and used every tool available to her over the years. From the start, her best tool came from the knowledge that her fulfillment would only come from herself. She used the term "icing on the cake" to describe to herself her feelings about the fact that William had achieved the same mental and spiritual state as she.

She knew that even now, as he stood at the kitchen window, he was actively enjoying his view of their countryside and wore a slight smile in recognition of his enjoyment.

Soon she would get up and begin the evening. The sunlight now had the yellow cast of late afternoon, redecorating the white-walled hallways and rooms from the whiter light of midday. Conversation would begin. Sounds that had slept through the day would now awaken. A twilight drive down white birch-lined lanes would reveal new sights as others were receding, the luminescent trunks of the trees being the sights that receded last. And later, as night became established throughout the area, whippoorwills would call in their low, solitary whistle.

~~~

But now it's late afternoon, and in the moment it takes for this recognition, my mind pulls back from this scene and I'm alone in my office. These thoughts and feelings, these sights and sounds, all coalesced in only the time it took to glance up from the work on my desk to look through the window and out towards the sunlight lowering on the horizon.

It was the quality of the light, yellowish in its shading, and the billowy whites of the clouds floating in the blue sky that I think set my short afternoon-dream in motion. A kind of deja vu experience.

Wishing to keep hold of the scene, I try desperately to connect it with some event or moment that I've actually had in the past. Or maybe I just saw the scene, or one similar, as an illustration on the face of a postcard.

Whichever it may be, it makes me catch a breath, as though I were coming out of a transcendental experience. Almost as quickly as the vision emerged, it faded. Despite my protests. Because I didn't want it to go. Fortunately for me, these sensory episodes are happening on a more regular basis; there will be more. They usually cause lonely, longing feelings in me but for some reason, I like that. And I think in some way, for other reasons that I don't know, I *need* those feelings.

I HAVE RHINOCEROS HANDS
The Vignette

Moonlight reveals but a fraction of the severity of texture on my hands and arms. To look at me, you would be able to feel me, as she feels me now. There is only one part of me that has not the scaling, dirt brown thickness. That is the part of me that is within her, alive and on its own.

I have rhinoceros hands. And arms. And stomach, back, legs and feet. I've become this way from merely living. All my life I have held dirt and mud and all manner of earthy substance and have brought it to my parts, smudged with glue and doused with water and rain and spit.

When I was much younger – I am not old now, though to look at me unmoving you would think me extremely old – there was a time in which I was working to remove the accumulation of this leathery coat. I felt it was not – should not be – a part of me and therefore didn't want to share it with anyone, or more exactly, thought that no one should be made to suffer its effects. I tried all manner of peeling, sanding, scraping, and smoothing to lessen its visual and tactile severity. All to no avail. Everything that I engaged in brought more of the stuff to me. So I gave up, I let go.

I learned to like the sensation of holding handfuls of dirt and debris and mixing it with glue and sometimes my own saliva, kneading it and squashing it between my fingers, and finally spreading it out myself on my own body. Oh, to feel it hardening, still keeping its gluey elasticity, tightening itself over my own original skin until it embedded itself in my pores and within its own cracks and fissures. It became my armor!

As I push and nudge against her own smooth and supple skin, here in the very early morning, I can see the softness becoming red with the abrasiveness. Her eyes are open and looking right at me. An acceptance of what I have to give is what she is exhibiting through her eyes. To be sure, she can see who and what I am and how I look, and still she moves with me. We part our lips to kiss and, with a flick, my tongue touches her lips, its soft wetness almost a shock to her. But it is not a shock, she knows who I am and what I am about, my tongue being an incongruity similar to that other part of me that is inside her, the part that is hidden when not in use and hidden when in use so that it has never known the accumulation that the rest of my body has known. And she knows me through this part.

Still watching me, she wraps herself tighter to me. I know that this must increase the friction between our surfaces, but I continue because it's what she wants. And I want it as I move us more rapidly to our conclusion. We finish and there is only heaviness of breathing in the silence of the moonlight. I stand to look at her laying there, body bruised and scraped, sweat mixed with crumblings of my hide on her rising and falling torso, and she appears used. As I stand there against the night-lit curtain, air touching me through the cracks and crevices of my rhinoceros skin, she is still looking at me with eyes I know through which she is somehow, miraculously, fulfilled.

I wonder how this can be and how I can have such good fortune to have been able to give what I can to this other. I wonder what the next moment will hold, and the next and the next. As I wonder all that I can wonder, she rises, comes to me, and brings me around to face the moonlight – she now can see the full extent of my bodily texture – and there is a light on her face and body that does not come from the moon, does not come from me, but is her own.

As she lifts her hand to my chest, I notice that in addition to the look of fulfillment in her eyes, she is smiling as she begins to gently peel the layers of covering back above my heart.

There, beneath the baked soil and clay which she carefully removes in small, brittle pieces, is a beautiful, luminescent blue! I look back and forth between my body and her eyes as she reveals more and more of this new, incredible me, not daring to believe what I truly am seeing.

The air is sweet on my new self! I can see the glowing blue reflected in her eyes as she looks up from her performance to check on me to make sure I am all right with all of this that is happening. Of course I am all right and as the moon becomes the sun she finishes, the two of us standing amid the mound of cast-off clods of second skin, holding each other tightly, the glowing blue evolving to a radiant pink enveloping us both.

SEPTEMBER

I smell September in the air as I run down the sloping hill, the new, white kite string in my small hand. The kite only twirls and twirls, its yellow rag tail grazing the ground each time it passes. Drying grass and its anchor of dirt puffs up around my ankles and settle in my pants cuffs.

September brushes against the skin on my arms, blows through my red hair and into my ear turned down toward the bottom of the hill, my eyes upward, watching the kite until I arrive, puffing and wheezing and letting the air pass through my vocal cords to give tone to my body coming to rest.

I am so grateful for being out in the open. I could not stand to be under a tree or on a porch when there's a sky overhead like the one I own at this moment.

Turning back up the hill for what must be the fourteenth time, I spool the kite string back onto the small piece of branch. I pick up my home-fashioned red diamond.

Reaching the top of the hill again and dropping my kite and kite string spool, I stick both hands into my pockets, fishing for my little knife. It's not in my right pocket, so I concentrate on the left, first bringing out my balled-up handkerchief; a clothespin left from helping mother with the laundry; my bright blue pinky squirt-gun; then loose change amounting to seventy-three cents; the small, mother-of-pearl-handled knife among the bright coins cupped in my palm.

I stuff all of the items back into my pocket and hold the knife in the fingers of both hands, inspecting. I loved that knife. Uncle

Roger loved it too, before he gave it to me. Shifting the knife to my right hand, I slide it into my right pocket, turning it over and over, feeling the smooth, flat sides and the humps of the two blades and I look out to the horizon.

I am surrounded by September. I would have to walk through all of twenty minutes worth of September to get home, which appears as a small white cube down toward the trees with the creek running through them. What if I had all day to walk down that side of the hill? Not even all the way home – just down the hill, through the grass and clover gone to seed, past the groundhog mounds and the tern's nest in the thistle bush with the small, putty egg shells recently broken open – robbed by a skunk. What else would I find there in my land of five hundred, fifty paces with hours and hours to cover the distance (a snail's pace by a human's standards)?

Like the grass anchored by the dirt, I am anchored by Uncle Roger's knife held between my curled fingers, palm, and thumb covered over the end. But yet I am determined to move and picking up my kite, I step one step and then another, taking all the time in the world to locate myself in one new place after another.

I am reminded of Uncle Roger's sea voyages and I look to my left as I step. His horizon was flat, featureless except for the endless waves bobbing up and down, calling to him and leading the way to his next destination. Another step and I am packing with Uncle Roger in his small studio apartment off the main part of the house. He stands with his steel-rimmed glasses and graying crew-cut; pudgy fingers holding his note cards, the tremor in his hands visibly shaking the paper.

Standing close to him – close to his dark blue wool jacket and the warmth it provides me – he crosses off each item packed in his hard-shell Samsonite suitcase. Concern for him fills my heart. I stand closer to him. The lines he draws are jagged and crooked, and reflect the instability of the flesh, nerves, and muscles of his hand. All of his writing is this way and I imagine him writing each letter rolling down railroad tracks in a car without tires and how my own teeth would clatter were I riding with him.

Step. A land mine explodes and grasshoppers take short flight in front of me and land, only to be launched again and again. September cuts the air with its high buzz-saw cicada-song, pulls me to a stop, and I again attempt to decode the rise-and-fall tempo of its drone. It is a mystery of sound.

I yank my shirt from the elastic waistband of my pants, reach in along the inside to feel the ridges of skin the tightness has made and rub back and forth for relief. I think of all of the things that bring that feeling of relief, like letting the air escape my lungs, through my throat with sound, after an extreme effort. Like running home from playing down the road when it's turned dark and finally grasping the screen door handle up on the porch. And the relief of finally sitting down, supplied with buttered popcorn, soda-pop, and a slow-poke sucker in a cool, dark movie theater after having waited through morning chores and then a long line in the afternoon sun when you could have done a million other things.

And the glad relief I felt the year before, running home from the school bus stop and finding Uncle Roger's round-nosed and chrome-fitted Buick with its freshly pressed-out tire tracks in the dirt and the knowledge that *now* I would find out the details of Moroccan market stall trading only hinted at in postcards sent weeks before but only recently received.

I am tempted to sit down in the dirt, I'm moving so slowly down the hill, but September coaxes me on. I raise my leg in slow motion, swing my arms at the same tempo until I can't anymore and I have to put the next foot down and leap off of it to land in a mushroom cloud of dust three feet further into the desert of Northern Africa, standing before the gates of the Chella Necropolis Cemetery that Uncle Roger described to us in historical detail.

I would watch his eyes fill with the worldliness and irony of his voyages out and returns homeward – his longing for experience and knowledge always approximal with his love of family; his growing infirmity; his love of me. He would tell us – Father and Mother and my two brothers – of when he had been in the capital of Rabat and had been invited by a prominent businessman with whom he had met on another of his trips abroad, to a celebration at the King's palace. He knew that I would keep the secret that the stories told were for me, chiefly; that *he* knew I was the one who would appreciate them most.

The Moroccan trip was the last one that Uncle Roger took. I am now the one to forage out – the one to keep Uncle Roger's tradition alive; the one to make my packing lists; keep stationary to send to family and friends; carry personal business cards to hand out; and the one to keep the little mother-of-pearl knife, in its soft suede slipcase, at the ready for the next voyage.

Exasperated in remembering I have to go back and get the kite, I run again, laboring under the looming finality of a spent September afternoon, not wishing to know that I have to go on from here.

"Let's see that fine red kite you have there.", Uncle Roger says to me when I finally arrive, to *his* relief, at the bottom of the hill after what seems like hours since I ran up it at top speed the first time, fifteen minutes before.

"I believe you have to have a little more weight on that tail. We'll put some more of this old yellow tablecloth your mother gave us on it."

September holds us both in its airy-sweet, loving arms as Uncle Roger tears the yellow cloth with his trembling hands and ties it to the rag tail, ensuring its flight now.

I stand closer to him.

I HAVE RHINOCEROS HANDS
The Story

"Okay, my name is Kevin O'Donnell. I'm twenty-five, last week, by the way. Um, I work at the Perfex plant – I'm a brake press operator. I been divorced about five years. I don't know if that's what I'm s'posed to say. Is it?"

"That's fine, Kevin. Do you know what you're here for?" asked Dr. Shalit.

"It's either because of my accident directly or it's about what caused it. I guess. I don't know. The insurance company told me I had to do it to make a claim. Do you know?"

"Well, first off, I do know that the personal psychological evaluation that you went through with Dr. Nalls had to do with your insurance claim – I thought he would've made you aware of that. As for this group therapy, it's mainly to get you through the trauma that you've experienced – and, again, it's all strictly confidential here, you can say anything you like. Let's do a little talking and maybe we'll find out what's going on with you. Okay?"

"Sure, Kev," Tony put in, "spill your guts so they can turn that workers comp claim around. Then they don't have t'pay nothin'. "

"That's right!" agreed Larry.

"Don't worry about that, Kevin," assured Dr. Shalit, "it's past that point. These discussions will have no bearing on your claim. Go on."

"I guess the first thing is that I had my first dream when I stopped seein' this one girl that I thought was the one. Right. That was about ten years ago. They – the dreams – came once in a while after that until I got the brake press job last year, then they started comin' 'bout once a week during work. Maybe it was the routine that did it, I guess."

"What's a brake press?" asked Nathan.

"It's a machine kinda like a big commercial paper cutter but you use it to bend big pieces a metal," Tony offered.

"You run one?" asked Kevin.

"Tell us about the dream, Kevin," said Dr. Shalit.

"Okay, but I'm not any kinda speaker or anything like that, so gimme a break if it don't come out so it sounds like anything. I tried tellin' a good friend, Mark, about it but when I told him it just sounded weird the way it came out. I s'pose it didn't help that we were down at HoJo's at happy hour – it's not exactly a serious place."

"Unless you were seriously shit-faced!" said Tony.

"I could get seriously shit-faced right now," Larry said.

"Me too!"

The rest joined in.

"Anyway, what I know how to say ain't quite right with what I feel when this thing comes on. It's so much… bigger than the words I can use and it kinda feels like I'm gonna fuck it up – my memory of it- by tryin' ta talk about it. But, shit… well… I guess I don't have nothin' to lose."

"Not anymore, you don't, buddy," said Tony.

"So let's hear the thing, already," Ted urged.

"I can't describe the mood the way it was, but in this dream I'm feeling really tired and, you know, kinda weighed down with all this, uh, baggage is what they call it."

"Emotional baggage," offered Dr. Shalit.

"Right," continued Kevin. "And I'm in this room, at night… "

Moonlight reveals but a fraction of the severity of texture on my hands and arms. To look at me, you would be able to feel me, as she feels me now. There is only one part of me that has not the scaling, dirt brown thickness. That is the part of me that is within her, alive and on its own.

"What?"

"You're what?"

"Well, I'm fucking her. Okay? And I just feel like, Jesus, I don't know, like, you know when you feel like everything's wrong but you don't know what'd be right? Anyway, you feel real weird. And in the dream or vision or whatever… "

"How 'bout hallucination?"

"Flashback. I get 'em sometimes," Tony added. "Kinda think that's why I'm in this mess. Old lady turned me in. Said 'this boy's got ta get some help' but everybody in this group's fucked-up so I'm thinkin', maybe I'm normal."

"If you're normal, I'd hate to see fucked-up!" Larry laughed.

"Okay, okay," reminded Dr. Shalit. "Kevin, what if we called it a… fantasy? Would that work for you?"

"Sure, why not? But it really started out as a dream, remember. So, in this fantasy – it sounds stupid t' say fantasy, like it's Fantasy Island or some women's sex story… I'll stay with a dream – the only thing that I can figure about the way I look and stuff is I took this art course in community college and we had to do this project where we turn a drawing or something flat into something solid and I thought about a rhino. I looked it up in the encyclopedia and found a picture of one that looked like it had armor plates on it. Really tough and protected."

"But who's the chick?" asked Larry

"It's his old lady," Tony said with assurance.

"I don't have a old lady," Kevin corrected. "I don't know who it is and I can't figure this one out cause I never even met a woman like this one in the dream. I don't think one even exists... "

I have rhinoceros hands. And arms. And stomach, back, legs and feet. I've become this way from merely living. All my life I have held dirt and mud and all manner of earthy substance and have brought it to my parts, smudged with glue and doused with water and rain and spit.

"Oh, right," Tony said, "You're some sorta fuckin' rhinoceros-man. Shit. What kinda fucked-up shit is that?"

"Hey, Kevin, chicks really go for that big hard horn a yours, don't they?" Larry asked.

"Hey, guys, I said there were no restrictions on what was said here, but give Kevin a little slack. Kevin, keep talking. You've got a good imagination."

"Ha!"

"Shit!"

"Well I remember my art instructor telling me I had a good imagination when he saw how I was makin' the skin for the rhino. Out behind the building, I got some dirt from some new construction and mixed it with a whole lotta Elmer's Glue. I mixed it all up with my hands like makin' mud pies and spread it out on the pieces a plywood that I cut out in shapes like the rhino's armor. After about two days it was all dried an' cracked like a dried pond but it didn't fall off the plywood 'cause a all that glue.

"The thing that I liked more than anything about the project, was the way the mud with the glue in it dried on my hands... "

"Oh, wow, I remember," said Larry, "in grade school the way I'd pour glue all over my hand and let it dry and then keep adding layers until you had this other kinda skin that you peel off in one big piece with your fingerprints on it and everything! Yeah, I could do that all day."

"Cool."

"Anyway, anyway, it was great." Kevin continued. "After class one night, I was gonna go over to my girlfriend's house and mess around – we kinda planned this little sex scene that she got into – so I left the stuff on me. Couldn't get it off, anyways. Guys I knew told me about all the chicks they knew that got into weird stuff like bein' scared and dominated. Allison liked to have me be real forceful with her, but it kinda scared me – I didn't wanna go too far and have her get pissed off and think I was a creep. But I really liked the way my hands looked and felt so I figured she would, too. After so much mixin' up dirt and spreading it on, the mud and glue built up on my hands 'til it was about a half inch thick, and past my wrists… this high."

"Musta been like concrete, I bet," guessed Ted.

"It was really hard. You could rap on it with a screwdriver or somethin' and it'd make a knocking sound. But it bended and moved… "

When I was much younger – I am not old now, though to look at me unmoving you would think me extremely old – there was a time in which I was working to remove the accumulation of this leathery coat. I felt it was not, should not be, a part of me and therefore didn't want to share it with anyone, or more exactly, thought that no one should be made to suffer its effects. I tried all manner of peeling, sanding, scraping, and smoothing to lessen its visual and tactile severity. All to no avail, though. Everything that I engaged in brought more of the stuff to me. So I gave up, I let go.

"… then I guess at some point a few years ago I said screw it, why do I wanna be so different from all my friends? Where did it get me? Besides, it's guys like you, Tony, that get laid all the time anyway."

"Hold everything here, Jack. What the hell are you tryin' to say?" Tony challenged.

"I'm not sayin' that you're this bad, but… don't most women go for guys that treat 'em like shit anyway?"

"Whoa!" Larry cautioned.

"Even Tony shouldn't have to take that slam," Nathan protested.

"Just what the fuck do you know about how I treat women anyway, asshole? Fuckin' Rhino-man!"

"Hey, I'm sorry. Okay?" defended Kevin. "Maybe it's just me who treats 'em like they didn't deserve any respect. Maybe it's just me."

"Yeah, maybe!"

"Yeah, and maybe it's just me who never gets any respect from them, neither," said Kevin. "Maybe I feel I gotta beat 'em to the punch just to protect myself."

"Sorry, Kevin," Dr. Shalit came in, "but you just don't seem the type of man to be mean and disrespectful to women. I could be wrong, I don't think so, though."

"Maybe I'm not," Kevin said, "but I *think* about being that way. I mean, sometimes it'd feel real good to just haul off and smack some broad when she's comin' off like it's all my fault for every shitty thing some guy's done to her. That's what was goin' on in my head usually when I was at work and thinkin' about not bein' with a girl that night, the way it was most nights. It was just fine by me, though… "

I learned to like the sensation of holding handfuls of dirt and debris and mixing it with glue and sometimes my own saliva, kneading it and squashing it between my fingers, and finally spreading it out myself on my own body. Oh, to feel it hardening, still keeping its gluey elasticity, tightening itself over my own original skin until it embedded itself in my pores and within its own cracks and fissures. It became my armor!

"Kevin, did you ever go over to your girlfriend's? With your hands like they were?" asked Dr. Shalit. "You didn't mention whether you did or not."

"Yeah, what about that?" asked Tony.

"Yeah, I think we forgot about that," Larry said.

"Tell us," they all demanded.

"I don't think I wanna talk about that," said Kevin.

"I think by the same token that we don't restrict anything in our discussion here, Kevin, we don't want to hold anything out, either," the doctor argued.

"Oh, right," Kevin came back, "it's easy for you to say, you don't have the same kinda shit comin' down in your rosy little life, you don't have anything eatin' you up inside. You got it made, you can even shrink yourself!"

"Bingo," said Tony.

"Don't be so sure about that, guys," Dr. Shalit offered. "But you still need to talk about what happened with your girlfriend. We'll all promise not to give you a hard time about it, won't we guys?"

"Okay, okay," surrenders Kevin, "it don't matter anyway, it's history. She's long gone. Like the lady in the dream… "

As I push and nudge against her own smooth and supple skin, here in the very early morning, I can see the softness becoming red with the abrasiveness. Her eyes are open and looking right at me. An acceptance of what I have to give is what she is exhibiting through her eyes. To be sure, she can see who and what I am and how I look, and still she moves with me. We part our lips to kiss and, with a flick, my tongue touches her lips, its soft wetness almost a shock to her. But it is not a shock, she knows who I am and what I am about, my tongue being an incongruity similar to that other part of me that is inside her, the part that is hidden when not in use and hidden when in use so that it has never known the accumulation that the rest of my body has known. And she knows me through this part.

"So you've come into Allison's house and she's got every single light off, and she's left a trail of her clothing towards the bedroom?" asked Dr. Shalit.

"Yeah, she did that one other time. Well, with me, at least."

"Uh-huh," said Tony.

"Come on, get on with it already," insisted Ted.

"By the time I get to her bedroom, I'm like, almost shakin' 'cause of the dark and it's all quiet and she knows I'm coming but she don't know I got these rhinoceros hands and I know she's gonna go bananas and screw my brains out when she sees 'em.

"And so I get next to the bed and she's laying there, on her front pretendin' to sleep – with nothin' on – so I reach down and just grab hold of her sides real solid-like and she screams so loud I can't hear for a second. I remember standin' straight up with my hands out in front of me and thinkin' 'Jeez, you were asleep!'. But from then on it's just like I was in outer space in a space suit tryin' to figure out what's going on down on earth… "

Still watching me, she wraps herself tighter to me. I know that this must increase the friction between our surfaces, but I continue because it's what she wants. And I want it as I move us more rapidly to our conclusion. We finish and there is only heaviness of breathing in the silence of the moonlight. I stand to look at her laying there, body bruised and scraped, sweat mixed with crumblings of my hide on her rising and falling torso, and she appears used. As I stand there against the night-lit curtain, air touching me through the cracks and crevices of my rhinoceros skin, she is still looking at me with eyes I know through which she is somehow, miraculously, fulfilled.

"… and so, through all this cussin' and yellin' at me, I can't even say one word."

"She's standin' there, tits and all, callin' you every dirty name in the book, and you can't say nothin'?" said Larry.

"Nope."

"Pussy!" called Ted.

"Kevin's right," Tony said to Ted, " sometimes you just gotta chill out when everything's stacked against you."

"Did you know who the guy was?" asked Dr. Shalit.

"Nope, never seen 'im," answers Kevin. "And I sure didn't see him lyin' there underneath Allison 'til she jumped up and started beatin' on me. He didn't say anything – just sat up in her bed and took in the show… "

I wonder how this can be and how I can have such good fortune to have been able to give what I can to this other. I wonder what the next moment will hold, and the next and the next. As I wonder all that I can wonder, she rises, comes to me and brings me around to face the moonlight – she now can see the full extent of my bodily texture-and there is a light on her face and body that does not come from the moon, does not come from me, but is of her own.

"… next thing I know, I'm driving home, not even seeing the road – like I was on autopilot. Jesus, you know, I just thought about it now, that's just about exactly how I feel when I'm havin' one a these dreams at work. Especially the last time."

"So," Dr. Shalit asked, "did anyone try to talk to you while you were feeling this way?"

"No," replied Kevin.

"Why not?"

"It was really noisy so nobody tried to make any kinda conversation – that was for break-time. Plus, I think I kinda looked like I didn't want anybody to talk to me."

"How so?"

"Well, I remember goin' in the washroom during one of the dreams – the last one – and lookin' in the mirror after washing my hands after takin' a whiz and I couldn't see me in the mirror... "

As she lifts her hand to my chest, I notice that in addition to the look of fulfillment in her eyes, she is smiling and she begins to gently peel the layers of covering back above my heart.

"... only on that day, it was worse than ever and I was really tired 'cause I didn't get a whole lotta sleep the night before – really shitty dreams – and I was really fed up with havin' this thing keep remindin' me of something that wasn't never gonna be- not to mention worrying about havin' it mess up my job. I remember thinkin' that I kinda remembered that I came to some resolution or decision or something the night before. Now I know it was about doing somethin' to change things... ."

There, beneath the baked soil and clay which she carefully removes in small, brittle pieces, is a beautiful, luminescent blue! I look back and forth between my body and her eyes as she reveals more and more of this new, incredible me, not daring to believe what I truly am seeing.

"... and it was like watching myself from right next to me, workin' the press and feelin' good like I usually do in that part of the dream and thinking, 'Yep, I'm gonna change things'. Watchin' myself move and dreaming... "

The air is sweet on my new self! I can see the glowing blue reflected in her eyes as she looks up from her performance to check on me to make sure I am all right with all of this that is happening. Of course I am all right and as the moon becomes the sun she finishes, the two of us standing amid the mound of cast-off clods of second skin, holding each other tightly, the glowing blue evolving to a radiant pink enveloping us both.

"… and that's when I kinda came to, when the press came down and all that blood spurtin' everywhere, in my face, in my eyes. 2000 pounds per square inch is what we were told it put out. My fingers were just like little sausages to that press and with the back-pressure plate, there wasn't no place for all that blood t'go – except all over me – goddamn, it hurts where they were. It's weird."

"No shit, fucking gruesome!" Tony said.

"I'd say it's weird!" Nathan said.

"No," corrected Kevin, "What's weird is I stopped havin' the dream right from that point."

"Case closed, Dr. Ruth," Larry proclaimed.

"Dr. Shalit?" asked Kevin.

"What, Kevin?"

"Do you do hypnosis?"

"Why?"

"I miss them."

"Kevin, I know it's going to be extremely difficult getting your mind and the rest of your body to accept that your fingers are g…"

"No! That dream – those dreams. It's all I had – I want 'em back."

POOL OF SOULS

"Brick-a-brick-a-brick-brack-brick. Toledo torpedo skoondama moona. Tulips in spring and silk in your ear, bring me back a baby who is not so near!" called Russell with an "open sesame" cadence to the blackbirds out on the grassy median. The lady in the apartment underneath his stuck out her head-turned-upward and blew him a big puckered-up kiss. She always reminded him of Rosie, his great aunt's cigar-smoking maid.

Russell ducked back in from the open window as though she had never seen him.

"You sure are a handsome blue-eyed devil, Rusty!", Pyrena teased. "I think you ought ta come down here for some iced coffee right this instant." She didn't expect him to come down – he never would – but she liked to keep that invitation open to this man who never seemed to have time to sit and yap with her but always had "interested" in his eyes.

Russell caught black movement to his left and quickly lowered the screen as Ellen, his cat, was on her way towards flight out the second-story window. Not having much ledge to grab onto, she fell off sideways, her claws scraping for purchase. She landed awkwardly and padded off with embarrassment to the back of the apartment where she had a carpeted ledge Russell had erected at the window for her.

"Sorry, Ellen," he called to her, hoping she wouldn't hold it against him too long. Russell Terbeck turned back to the kitchen window that he had chosen this particular apartment for. The late afternoon light graphically painted its way in across the gloss white wall and canary yellow Formica table. Jumping across the floor and out into the living room, it appeared superimposed with even whiter dust motes floating in the dark spaces of light.

Russell picked up his tin can of iced coffee and swallowed once. He decided to go ahead and sit down at the table to look out toward the street for an extended time of at least fifteen minutes. Postponing his nap time didn't bother him and it would get him over to Fenneman's after the crowd. He didn't feel like socializing this evening with the other retirees who usually made conversation with him. Elaine Wenzel would undoubtedly show up and exclaim, "It's always so crowded in here!" She would ask him if he "… wouldn't mind sharing his table with a lady?" while sliding his side dishes of green beans and spoonbread into his entrée dish of meatloaf and mashed potatoes. Russell thought, *"Where was the Order in Life when you were put into the pot with a Sagittarian?"*

In the largest of trees out across the street, Russell visualized a face in the pattern of leaves. It wasn't Elaine Wenzel's. It was another Sagittarian's face – Valida's. Immediately rising from the table, Russell went to the sink, dumped out the remaining coffee and rinsed the tin can thoroughly, placing it on the red wire drainer. He made two steps to the window, grabbed the venetian blind cord and yanked it so that the blinds lowered with a clatter to the sill, and walked stiffly out through the living room to his bedroom.

In there, the light was muted except for some reflection from the next building in the complex. Russell went to stand before the full-length mirror attached to the closet door and examined the small three-by-five-inch color prints and assorted Polaroids that framed the upper portion of the mirror. His eyes wandered from image to image, intentionally avoiding a specific photo that he always saved for last.

Most of the pictures were of himself, differentiated by styles of clothes, length and amount of hair, various vehicles included in the photo, and marked in time by where the picture was taken. A few were of himself and a friend or old girlfriend. Before Russell's eyes came to that one particular print, he brought his gaze to the center of the ring of photos to find his current self glaring back with a deeply furrowed brow.

Because no one looked on, Russell allowed himself to look into the mirror to try and determine what he looked like to himself and to others. He saw thinning hair – almost bald, really, a roundish face with fewer lines than another man his age of fifty-seven, and he saw a body he did not remember possessing. *"Did I time travel to this condition?"* he thought. Letting out his breath, Russell saw his midsection stretch out his blue shirt, smoothing out the dry cleaner creases. It caused him to grimace as though he were being confronted by an injection needle. He turned to observe his profile and ridiculed himself with the thought, *"If my gut gets any bigger, it'll look like I have an ass coming and going!"* He promptly removed his bloated wallet and vowed never to "mess up the lines" with it again. Russell saw a man who was someone other than Russell Terbeck. It was a difficult thing to look at himself so he screwed up his face absurdly and threw the closet door open to hide the mirror. It slammed against the wall and the picture that he could not look at fluttered to the floor underneath his bed, even as he was walking out without having taken his late afternoon nap.

Ellen had been there at the door looking in, and now ran after and ahead of him for attention. He stopped to pick her up and scratch behind her ears but as soon as she was in his arms, she growled and pushed against him, jumping to the floor.

"Bitch, Rat Face." he threw after her. Ellen had been found outside of the Arlington Heritage Museum by a lady friend working as assistant curator in the dead of winter ten years back. She was just a kitten and had been abandoned. Russell wanted a little unconditional loving and had thought that taking the kitten in would be the simplest way to get it. He now called Ellen his "lesson in commitment". Russell wished he had it in him to give her a kick as he walked by on the way to the door, but only told her goodbye as he lifted his apartment keys from the key hook and left for Fenneman's.

~~~

Russell had been living for the past twenty-one years in an older brick apartment building in Falls Church, Virginia, not far from Washington, D.C. It was in a large and sprawling complex with plenty of trees and grass and known as Mormon Hill in reference to its owners, and was a quiet place amid a congested area called Seven Corners. The rent was reasonable for the D.C. area and the upkeep good, with the advantage of being on a major bus route. And this time, he was allowed to keep Ellen, which Russell regretted on occasion. Xavier DeSilva, a Mormon converted from Catholicism by his Louisiana wife, had recommended the apartments to him when Russell had moved to the D.C. area once before while in his early twenties. Mr. DeSilva had been his department supervisor and had taken Russell under his wing, hoping to keep him there long enough to have Russell take over for him. Russell became restless, though, and had moved back to the Midwest after only two years.

That was when Valida came into his life. She was twenty- two, and a woman with the youthfulness of a girl. Everyone noted how good they were together – two peas in a pod, Romeo and Juliet, brother and sister, Ying and Yang, and on down the line so much so, that Russell could not even think of the two of them being apart. And Valida was beautiful, not just in his eyes, but in others' as well. But she was a Sagittarian – loyal in the affair, fickle about commitment and enthusiastic about life, loud in style. Russell was both infatuated and angry with her, alternately, and this only contributed to their passionate relationship. She was something! Life was not boring when he was with her.

Because of his youth, his lack of emotional experience, and a generous helping of self-denial of reality and his own challenges, it drove him crazy. Both to not have her as a sure thing and at the same time, to not want her in her entirety. He felt the only way out was for her to marry him. Then he would have all of the things he loved and not be able to run from the things he didn't.

Russell had given Valida the ultimatum back in Des Moines. After Valida had refused to marry him, he moved back east and out of reach of those memories. He blamed her for her choice. The blame and the loss had twisted his heart so badly, he had run away, marked by pain from a continual rehashing of the what if's, the why's, and the final placing of blame to assuage his failure to stay and work on the relationship as it was. It had thrown an ocean of water onto his flame of passion and spontaneity.

Russell walked along the sidewalk that ran between the buildings and across the grass behind the complex to the Seven Corners Shopping Center, just to the rear of the complex. Coming out onto the asphalt parking lots, he could see that the big silver letters of Fenneman's were already lit up from behind for the evening's patrons.

Looking down at his feet moving and walking along the faded yellow line that ran down the middle of a row of empty parking spaces, Russell thought of Mr. DeSilva. Before he died, Mr. DeSilva had to have his right foot amputated because of severe gangrene caused in part by the diabetes that finally took his life. He used to ask Russell to give him a ride home from the office to stop and have dinner at Fenneman's. Mr. DeSilva's wife, Lorretta, would meet them there at the cafeteria for her night off from cooking. When she cooked, she cooked up a feast! Russell had eaten many meals cooked by Mrs. DeSilva after helping Mr. DeSilva around the house.

He had enjoyed a unique relationship with Mr. DeSilva that no one in the cartographic department could claim. Not that anyone wanted to – DeSilva was a cranky Peruvian and as big a man as any at six-three and a good two hundred-eighty plus pounds. He had pride to match and was in disagreement with virtually everyone except the other two South Americans he supervised.

They were simply overpowered by his quick, Latin-tongued intellect. Mr. DeSilva had come to the U.S. from Peru, where he had been a chief mapping expert in the jungles. Despite DeSilva's extensive knowledge of cartography, Russell found himself challenging his authority for the sake of the challenge.

"According to the aerial photo, the road here makes a bend. I think I should ink it as it appears." Russell began.

"Listen, *Gringo Sin Verguenza*, there is no need to draw this road with every little pothole that you see in the photo. Just draw the straight line," said DeSilva in his clipped Latino English.

"How can I *not* do what I see should be done?" continued Russell. "You want me to draw a four-way intersection instead of a cloverleaf interchange just because you want me to save a few minutes in the budget?"

"*Carajo, Burro Blanco,* if you don't want to do as I tell you to do, just sit there and do nothing!" growled DeSilva, shaking a big, yellowed and split-nailed finger at him. Russell sat there doing nothing until break time. Once on break, the two of them hashed it out until DeSilva privately gave in when Russell presented his argument of not wanting to slack off like most of the other gringos in the office.

"Okay, Gringo, you can do the good job for once on this map and screw *el Jefe* if it goes over the budget. *Los Dios* knows I don't have anyone to produce a new map since before you came here. They give all the maps to the *hijo de puta* negative cutters that live in the dark."

"Gracias, el Patrón de boles." mocked Russell.

Mr. DeSilva then lowered his voice and deigned to look with his pale, clouded eyes directly at Russell and asked, "Listen, can you come to my house on Saturday?"

Russell answered "Sure." without thinking.

"Good, I have some things that need to be done and my dear wife will not let me do them. My foot is not doing so hot so she wants to me to take it easy this weekend. What a load of *mierda*, huh, Gringo?"

"No problem, I can come."

"What does she think, that I cannot get it up like this? Like a stallion?" DeSilva raised his beefy, stiffened forearm with his big ball of a fist clenched and trembling from the nerve damage.

That Saturday morning at nine o'clock, the twenty-one-year-old Russell drove over to Alexandria to Mr. DeSilva's house. DeSilva was there on the porch in paint-splattered slacks and a green open-necked shirt readying the materials for the work. He greeted Russell with an inspecting eye and pronounced "Too much pussy last night, Gringo. I can tell by the way you are dragging your ass!" And DeSilva shuffled around the room, shoulders slumped, mouth drooping and eyes almost shut. They had a good laugh and DeSilva lined up the work for the morning. The porch would be painted first and then if there was time, they would go over to Hechinger's for some lumber and nails to frame up the azalea garden.

Painting went quickly and the two of them returned from the lumber yard in Russell's gray primer-spotted Toyota which was seriously listing to the passenger side from the weight of the gigantic man and the stack of two-by-fours red-flagged and hanging out the back.

"Lunchtime, Burro Blanco," DeSilva yelled as he punched Russell in the arm. In the kitchen, Mr. DeSilva's wife was busy piling the table full of food.

"Hello, Russell. Are you hungry?" asked Lorretta, as Russell imagined DeSilva and his wife going to it "using every square foot of the house" as DeSilva claimed. *"What a license for screwing,"* he thought, *"Latin blood and the Mormon religion."*

"I save my hunger up for the whole week when I know I'm going to be here," said Russell.

"Good, we like to sit and watch you eat. You do such a good job of it. Here, start with this chicken casserole I made up this morning." commanded Lorretta. Along with the casserole, there was fresh three-bean salad; potato rolls; sweet potatoes with marshmallows, butter and brown sugar; celery-sage dressing; lemonade; iced tea; and of course, Diet Pepsi for Mr. DeSilva. Russell could only wonder at what might be for dessert.

Mr. DeSilva was rolling up his sleeve and preparing for his insulin injection when he said to Russell, "Which one did you have last night, the redhead? Or was it Dee-Dee? Or do you have another one we don't know about?"

"Xavier!" scolded Lorretta. "What kind of talk is that at the table?"

"Russell is the one who came in looking like he was in the meat grinder all night... are you jealous?"

Lorretta slapped DeSilva on the back of his head and gave Russell a look of apology and went to the stove.

Russell leaned over to DeSilva and whispered "I finally made it with Dee-Dee."

"Good," said DeSilva, "always keep the options open. If one gives you the ultimatum, you have another one to go to."

Mrs. DeSilva came to the table with a steaming apple and mint cream cheese pie and set it down in the only open space on the table as she sat after removing her apron and led the three of them in Grace.

~~~

As Russell reached the inside mall entrance to Fenneman's, he flashed on the photo on his mirror of his last day at AAA, his last week in Virginia. In the picture, DeSilva and Crazy Paul Moody are standing, holding their sides in laughter. In the background across the vast fifth floor of the building, heads are looking up from their work. Some are laughing, others are frowning, and still more are staring in disbelief. Prominent in the foreground and the object of all the attention, is the back of Russell, perched atop his drafting chair.

Russell chuckled out loud and remembered how it all started. On the day before his last day of work, Crazy Paul Moody had circulated a cartoon that he had drawn approximately twenty-five years earlier while he was in his thirties. He presented it to Russell with everyone's signatures as a going-away gift and Russell was immediately inspired. On his last day, Russell warned DeSilva and Moody that he planned to reenact the cartoon. They could not believe it – it was too good to be true!

At the agreed-upon time – a half hour before quitting time – Jerry Heflin pulled out his camera and took his position behind Russell's table. DeSilva had provided Russell with an obsolete map and took up his position with Moody in a place where they would have a good view of what was going to happen.

With an unsuspecting audience of about seventy-five people throughout the department, Russell climbed up on his chair.

At the top of his lungs, he yelled, "I QUIT!!!" And as heads began popping up all down the floor, Russell squeezed hard on the yellow-water-filled honey bear hidden in his hands at groin level, a steady stream emptying out onto the map in front of him. Jerry Heflin snapped the photo, capturing DeSilva and Moody practically dying of laughter over the stream appearing to be coming from Russell, and Orr Raider, the disrespected department head, emerging from his end-of-floor office.

"He could've fired me over that one!" thought Russell as he entered Fenneman's Cafeteria. Once in line, he picked up his tray and set his silverware wrapped in a napkin onto it.

"A salad, this evening, Sir?"

"Yes," said Russell, sliding his tray down the line, "uh, I guess… uh, the… uh, hmm… ". *"Would the cucumber be better for me for the heat?"* thought Russell. "… the three bean, please." *"Vinegar. Crap, too late. Really, he couldn't have. I had quit already. "*

"What vegetable would you like, Sir?" asked the server.

I'll have… a, the… " Russell felt the push of people down the line behind him, "fried okra and the… mmm… Corn." *"Should've asked for the green beans! Did I do it only because it was safe?"*

"And what entrée can we offer you this evening, Sir?"

"Yes, I'll have the turkey breast. No, excuse me, give me the Polish sausage, please!" *"Jesus. What am I doing, I can't eat all this crap! What's my problem?"*

"A roll? Yes, thank you." *"And Valida. Was that safe? Or a wise choice? Or was it a choice at all?"*

Russell took an iced tea and paid the five dollars and forty-three cents for his meal, thinking, *"Don't think that. Of course it was my choice."* Picking up his tray, he swung around to head for the non-smoking section when CRASH!, Elaine Wenzel flopped right down onto her behind, her food splattering her entire front from the inertia, and a completely surprised and painful look on her face.

"Elaine, what the hell were you doing?" Russell blurted out, before the tears began to well up in her eyes.

"I forgot my Sweet-and-Low!" is all that she could say through her sobs as Russell, feeling the sting of his own guilt, moved quickly and proficiently to get as much food off of Elaine without either smearing it further or touching her breasts. He didn't succeed at either and Elaine pushed his hands away, accepting assistance from a busboy and regaining composure.

"Elaine, let me take you home." pleaded Russell.

"You don't have a car, are you going to fly me home?" she asked curtly.

"No, I do have a car," informed Russell.

"Go get it, then."

Russell ran as well as he could back across the parking lot to the back of his building where, under a cotton cover directly below the sodium vapor security light, his six-year-old Mercedes rested. Severely out of breath and sweating, Russell carefully rolled back the cover to reveal his gold-colored treasure.

"Oh, baby," he whispered as he stowed the cover in the trunk, contemplating the feel of the leather and the control of a machine much bigger than he.

This automobile was his endowment to himself upon the receipt of his first royalty check from Diebold Instruments. Diebold had bought Russell's patent rights for a new negative cutting software program used in mapping and other kinds of multi-colored computer-aided drafting. Russell had fallen in love with what he could get the computer to do and, being the supervisor in the mapping department this second time around at AAA, he had access and time enough to become proficient at it. He didn't actually like programming and he wasn't what you would call a computer nerd. He only learned enough to do what he wanted to do with it. With the initial sale of the invention, Russell had retired.

Elaine Wenzel's eyes visibly widened as Russell eased alongside the curb in front of Fenneman's. He got out and went to open the door for Elaine as she just stared at him.

She continued to stare as he got back in, buckled his seat belt, and finally looked up with a slight, sheepish smile.

"I guess I never told you I had a car," he admitted. "How do we get to your apartment?"

"Go up Leesburg Pike a bit. I'm just off it and I'm sure you put your hand on my breast intentionally," she stated.

"No, honest, I didn't. In fact, I tried to keep away from them." Russell quickly countered, following her directions.

"Why?" asked Elaine, still pinning him down with her eyes, "Do they frighten you?"

Russell took a moment from his focus on driving to see Elaine, her body turned toward him and a look of challenge in her eyes. "*Huh?*" he thought.

"Do I frighten you?" she pushed.

"*You sure as hell do. But not the way you may think.*" thought Russell as he was saying "Not in the least, I don't know what led you to think that."

"Come on, Russell, with all of these years socializing together… "

"We've been sitting together at a common table in the cafeteria and I am really sorry I knocked you over. I feel bad about it." injected Russell.

"In the first place," Elaine directed, "I ran into you. In the second place, this dress will clean up. And besides a sore butt and a bruised ego, I don't feel so bad about it. After all, Russell, I've gotten to see there's a bit more to you than any of us knew before. And I like what's hinted at. Take the next right."

Before he knew it, Russell was walking through Elaine's door into her apartment telling himself he shouldn't be doing so. Until that evening, Russell had always discouraged any discussion between himself and Elaine relating to personal relationships. Now Elaine had him in range.

"Please, don't pretend that you haven't shown the least bit of interest in me over these years of seeing and having conversations with each other," Elaine was saying after making a couple of salads and iced coffees for the two of them.

"Okay, I won't." complied Russell.

"Are you seeing anyone right now?"

"No, not really." He thought of Pyrena, an option.

"What the hell does 'not really' mean, Russell?"

"Okay, no one."

"Damn, I guess I'm going to have to yank all of your teeth to get anything out of you."

"No, it won't have to be so difficult. It's just that I know what I want and I don't have anything to hide so what do you want to know?" Russell asked.

"What would you like with me? Exactly."

"I suppose it depends on what you mean," answered Russell, running through about three different scenarios in his head.

"I'm not blind, Russell, I know you at least are interested in the way I look. You hide it well and for a man are pretty darn considerate, but come on, what else do you think about me?"

"Well, I'll be honest, I'd love to take you to bed. I hope you can take that as a compliment. But I'm just not sure I'd like to get any more involved than that."

"That's pretty damn involved, Russell. But you're open to whatever comes of it?"

Russell thought a moment. *"No, not whatever."* he thought. "Yes, I think so," he said. "But are you open to whatever may not come of things?"

They negotiated like this for another forty-five minutes through the salads and past the red grapes Elaine got out of the fridge. In the end, Russell followed Elaine into her bedroom, without brushing his teeth and without covering his Mercedes.

In the morning, Russell felt like a horse that's been standing asleep in his stall all night. After they had made love, which was worth staying for, Russell had lain in her bed mostly awake and partly okay with what had happened. His kidneys hurt from lying on his back having to pee too long. He inched his way out of her flowered and ruffled bed and into the rose sachet aroma-filled bathroom, sitting to urinate just as he thought she'd want, to assure that the seat remained down.

Afterward, Russell stood at the side of the bed examining Elaine's face while she still slept. Her head lay sideways on the bed – the pillow had been tossed away after she had used it to muffle her vocalizations – and her mouth was open with her cheeks smooshed together, one from the press of the bed, the other from gravity. Russell thought, "*If there were more to you for me, more that I was attracted to that I could fall back on, you wouldn't look so terribly unappealing right now.*"

"Come snuggle with me", Elaine asked, eyes still closed.

Russell slid beneath the sheets and into contact with Elaine. She buried her face in his graying chest. He looked down at the shape of her rear; to her feet with bunions turning her big toes inward; to her short, permed and colored hair-do. He gazed around the room from the panty-hose draped on the bed end to the cluttered dressing table, the double closet doors with racks containing thirty pairs of shoes with more racks on the floor of the closet, and to the dresser mirror with the reflection of the two of them – especially himself – reluctantly holding this other person and surrounded by all of that.

"I've got to get going, Elaine," Russell whispered, waiting for her concurrence.

"Really, you do?" she questioned, lifting her head to face him. "I thought I would fix us a big breakfast to replenish all that energy we spent last night. You look like you could use it."

"I'm sure I could. How about another time, though?"

She eyed him skeptically but flapped back the sheet anyway to allow his escape. "Okay, Russell. Just give me a call tonight to see how I'm doing. Make sure I'm not in crisis over this."

After Russell had dressed, they kissed and hugged each other sincerely. Elaine closed the apartment door whispering "Talk to you later… ", trailing it off for the desired effect.

Once in his car, Russell felt more himself. He eased the Mercedes out of the parking lot and fed the gas to it, steadily increasing his speed to bring his mind to the task of driving.

At the intersection of the street that he would turn left on to take him to his apartment, Russell made a right, having seen the sign for the carwash peeking out of the evergreens around the corner. He pulled into a bay, almost turning off the engine but pulling on through and leaving the carwash altogether. *"I can wash the car later,"* he thought, *"I have to get my shower and meditation in first."* Russell hated his car being dirty, and he could not put the cover back on until it was clean, but he hated himself not being clean inside and out even more. It was something of a dilemma for him.

Coming out of the bedroom in his undershorts afterward, letting out a big "Whew! Better!", Russell went looking for Ellen. She was sulking in the back room of the apartment on her ledge, and merely stretched in acknowledgment of her irresponsible keeper's return.

"Come on, Ellen, give me a break," Russell said as he picked her up, never giving up hope. Ellen responded to his deft scratches behind her ears by turning over her little purr-motor. This only lasted until Russell squeezed her to him and she snapped at his hand stroking her chin.

"Damn!" he said out loud. He then switched his hold of her and grabbed her by the scruff of her neck, holding her up in front of his face. Her ears flattened back to make her look even more rat-like.

"BE – NICE – TO – ME!" he yelled at her, trying once more to hold and pet her. She responded by digging her back claws into his ribs and forearm, thereby releasing his hold on her and escaping underneath the junk drawers.

Russell got down on all fours to look at her. She looked afraid and angry. He sat back onto the linoleum, thinking, *"I must have come out of meditation too fast."* But he knew something was eating at him underneath that hadn't been dissolved by the rest. Something big. He felt he had been in turmoil since yesterday, or the day before, or who knows how long.

Russell decided to look for a Daily Word for the proper perspective – it didn't matter which month, they were all the same, really. *"I seem to remember it being in Junk Drawer number six."* Russell thought. He went to it and jerked it open. It was the drawer containing all of his pins, emblems, and souvenir pieces of this and that. The cub scout neckerchief clasp that Russell had worn was near the back, pushed there by repeated insertions of more pieces into the drawer. He had only worn it until he was kicked out of Cub Scouts by the den mother for beating up her Cub Scout son.

He had liked that bright-polished gold clasp with the blue wolf's head in the middle. He liked the uniform and the routine of den meetings and treats and roughhousing in the wooded back yard. Ricky had been a jerk to him, though, picking on him because he could never make up his mind at anything. And only upon the teasing, incessant urging of the other boys to do something about it, he had, wrestling Ricky to the ground and punching him in the back and slapping his head until he cried to make him feel how Russell himself felt. Then he was kicked out, no longer able to be with his friends in that kind of context.

Russell went to Junk Drawer number nine, yanking it open to find pens and pencils to the brim. He decided to refer to his Junk Drawer List as there were twenty-six drawers filled, not to mention the stack of Timken Roller Bearing boxes that contained larger items like electrical parts and scraps of good wood. There was no listing for his Daily Words. He would have to look through the drawers until he found them.

"Maybe drawer number eight," he said to himself, pulling it all the way out of the cabinet because it stuck from the summer humidity. The drawer contained his screw driver collection.

"Where-is-the-Daily Word?" he said aloud, becoming angry. He shoved number eight so far back into the cabinet that he knew that if he didn't pull it back out then, he wouldn't get it open for the rest of the summer without doing damage to the cabinet. When he pulled it out this time, it flew out of his hands and landed on the floor, end up, spilling all the screwdrivers across the floor and sending Ellen off to other parts of the apartment.

"Fuck it!" he said without much restraint.

Russell shoved the tools across the floor with his bare foot and began yanking drawer after drawer, some flying to the floor, some not, until he realized that he'd seen his Daily Words out in his car in the trunk, ready to take to the Salvation Army.

Just then, his door buzzer rang.

"Jesus, didn't you see the sign not to use the buzzer?!" he growled.

As Russell walked out of the hallway and into the living room to peek through the peephole, in came Pyrena with a "Is everybody okay up here?!"

"Whoa! White bread has a name and it is Russell!" she exclaimed as soon as she saw Russell in his white Jockeys.

Russell quickly ran back into his room yelling, "Wait a minute, will you Pyrena?" and "How did you get in here?"

"The question is not *how* I got in here but *WHY* am I here?" she said going back towards his bedroom so they didn't have to talk long range. "You left your keys in the door so when I… "

Russell now emerged in pants and unbuttoned shirt, carrying a pair of his white work socks.

"Now that's a bit more respectable for a man of your age, Rusty. Not as interesting, but it'll do while you tell me if you're all right after all that commotion I heard up here. Thought that I was gonna have your apartment on my head."

"N', no, no, " Russell said, "Everything's fine. I left my keys in the door? I never do that!"

"You don't ever get out in the sun either, do you, now? So what was all that racket? You mind telling me?"

"There's not much to tell. A drawer fell out of the cabinet in back. It made a mess when it spilled – that's all." Russell lied.

Pyrena said in calmer voice, "Don't be B.S.'ing Pyrena, dear. I can see in your wild eyes and your trembling fingers that there's something wrong, something making you not your usual deliberate self. Maybe something wrong in your heart?" Pyrena tapped her chest. "Let's sit down in your kitchen here." She took him by the forearm and into the kitchen.

Russell thought it was something about the quality of her voice that made him feel like she knew what the hell she was doing and saying and he allowed himself to be led.

"Will you stay right here while I go get us something to drink?" she asked.

"I've got a mess to clean up back there. I really should get it cleaned up."

"Will you stay right here and let me do this for you?" she asked again, saying it slowly and looking directly into his eyes so he knew she meant it.

"Yes… thank you, Pyrena."

She left, leaving the door open and Russell went over to take his keys out of the lock. "*Not my deliberate self?*" he thought, going back to the table and sitting, pulling his socks on. He looked out of the window, the sun not yet winding its way down and around into his kitchen. "*Am I deliberate?*" he asked of himself.

He saw Valida's face in the tree across the way again and asked, "*Would she think I was deliberate?*" He felt anger and his breath quickening in his chest.

"I don't think so," he answered out loud. Russell looked at the clock. It was already two-thirty.

Pyrena Richards brought a whole tray full of things up to Russell's apartment. She had a steaming teapot, cups, cream, sugar, a basket of shortbread cookies, and a small dark bottle of something Russell had no idea of what was in it.

"We're going to fix you up good" she said.

Russell could smell chamomile and said, "I had in mind some of that iced coffee you're always inviting me for."

"Not in the state you're in today, honey. You need a little cooling down, not picking up. Rusty, there are things in this life that most people have not the teeniest clue about. Knowledge and wisdom we over here in the good old U.S. of A. refuse to see or listen to on account of we're so darn arrogant."

Amazed that Pyrena would have knowledge like that of which she was hinting, he only said, "I have an idea of what you're talking about, I would like to hear more."

Russell listened and it made sense to his logical mind. And in his logical mind, he started to pay more attention to Pyrena herself. He took in her physical appearance in even more detail than before. More than that, though, he observed his own ease in being with her and quite naturally took stock of the contrasts between she and Elaine, the woman most recently in Russell's life. And aside from the difference in race.

Pryena talked of Ayurvedic medicine from India and of other self-healing concepts she had gained during counseling sessions at a local women's center. She herself was employed at a drug rehab unit providing Personal Bill of Rights information to clients of the codependency group and seemed, to Russell, a model of self-confidence and verve.

"Boy, I wish that were right!" she said after Russell stated his observation.

"See, *I* thought I was doing just fine until this morning and now, geez, I feel that I may not be all serene and collected as I thought," Russell explained.

"And it's tough to even think that, right?" asked Pyrena.

"I guess it's easier talking to you," observed Russell, thinking how much he was beginning to like her.

"So talk to me about what's going on in you right now – if you want."

"I know one thing. I know I'm really angry. I can identify that much." said Russell.

"From what I know of you men, Rusty, you can usually get to the fact that there's something wrong, but identifying it much past anger or sadness or even happiness, you have a rough time doing."

"Right, well, suffice it so say that I just feel kind of mad. I've been mad at my cat and I've been mad at people in my life. I don't know why exactly but when I dumped a drawer out on the floor back there, I kind of just kept going." Russell could feel his emotions welling up inside his chest again. "Maybe I just need to get away for a bit."

"Yeah," Pyrena said, "sometimes a good clean break is just the thing."

Russell was settled somewhat by having someone agree with him and by his increasing fixation with Pyrena's mouth, her lips especially, and with her clear, round eyes moving in concert.

"Of course, " Pyrena said, noticing the extra intensity with which Russell paid attention, "it's always the first and easiest thing to do, change things outside of yourself."

"Meaning you think I would rather look elsewhere for answers than look at myself?" Russell asked, returning to the conversation.

"Ooo. You got my message. You're on the ball there ol' Rusty, my man."

"I think you and I have been going the same direction in our lives from what I can tell, Pyrena. And I don't think I'm that much older than you, you know."

"Well, we just won't make that an issue here, now will we?" instructed Pyrena. "Be good and drink up that tea, it should be cooled down by now." They drank the lukewarm tea and had a few cookies, Russell having more than a few as the sweetness might be a good thing for Russell, as Pyrena said.

"Pyrena, I just have to tell you something… " Russell started, wiping the crumbs from his mouth. She held up a hand.

"I don't want to hear that you're all fallen in love with me cause I brought you cookies and now you want to spread some of that sweetness around." she cautioned playfully.

"That's not what I was going to say even though it would be an ironic and fitting end to a bee-utiful afternoon, the sun lowering in the sky, the sounds of children in play outside, and you and I, finding each other here in the thick of the summer and having more than enough love to give to conquer the prejudice of others more ignorant than we." Russell managed to get out, running out of breath.

"What about all that anger? You going to give me some of that, too?"

"Okay, okay, I was going to tell you about my great aunt Jetta's maid – how you remind me of her."

"Oh, really?" Pyrena's eyebrows shot up at that one.

"Not that because you're black that you remind me of a maid… come on." defended Russell. "No, it was about how much I admired her. Her name was Rosie and she was there when we would visit my relatives down in Montgomery, Alabama. All my mother ever said about Rosie was that she wa a big colored woman, and 'she always was smokin' a big ol' cee-gar'".

Pyrena giggled.

"What I remember about her was that I always felt guilty for her having to pick up after us and wait on us at mealtimes and I was always profuse in my please and thank you's. I remember one morning we had eaten breakfast in the little alcove that was always filled with light and flowers and pink wallpaper and white iron chairs. My brothers and sister had gone away from the table and left me sitting, taking my time eating my second helping of cantaloupe that Rosie brought me.

Pyrena sat watching Russell who was looking out across the median into the trees while he spoke. She saw what he must feel in all of the times she had seen him looking out from that kitchen window by the way he cared for this story.

"I felt so good in that morning light. But every time Rosie entered to give me something or take dishes away, I felt guilty. As she took away my dishes after I had finally finished, I said, right out loud, 'I'm sorry you have to do this.'

"She looked angry for a second, then she smiled and sat down across from me and told me I didn't need to be sorry and I didn't have to go crazy trying to thank her for every little thing she did. Then she told me she liked what she did for a living and that between her and me, my Aunt Jetta had money, and that she paid her more than she probably should have. But the bottom line for her was that she enjoyed taking care of us and she enjoyed herself doing so.

"So. What I'll cut short to, is that this woman had a lot of... something... how can I say it... "

"Herself." Pyrena offered.

"Yes."

"Like I do?"

"Yes, that's what I feel about you," Russell said.

"And do you feel you have a lot of yourself?" she asked.

"I wasn't thinking about me. I wanted to say what I felt about you," he said.

"Is it difficult thinking about yourself?"

"Yes – no! I mean, why? There's so much else to think about." He remembered Elaine and Ricky, and Ellen's treatment of him. And Valida. Russell found himself getting uncomfortable again.

"Listen, Rusty, dear, I don't have much time left before I have to go. I'd really like to take care of one more thing. That tea should be making you sleepy – I remember you saying you have a routine rest in the late afternoon – so let's go have you sit in your chair in there for a little bit." She motioned towards the living room.

Russell was glad for the reprieve but was truly puzzled about what she had in mind. *"Maybe some more sexual relief?"* he fantasized. With the allure of that thought, Russell's mind and heart began to race.

Pyrena had him sit in his obviously well worn chair, kneeling before him on the floor.

"I'm in Heaven," Russell sang in his mind. *"… I'm in Heaven… I think I could fall deeply in love with this woman."* he thought as she brought out the dark bottle of oil, setting it down with a towel she took from his kitchen.

"Now you just sit back and receive this, Rusty, and trust me, I know what I'm doing," she said as she began taking Russell's socks off.

"Pyrena… " Russell said, cutting off his own thought of *"This is the woman for me!"* Then, "… what are you doing?"

Pyrena just raised her eyes up, then back down as she first rubbed her hands briskly together, then poured a small amount of the herbal smelling oil on her hands and began to massage Russell's virgin feet.

Reluctantly, Russell managed to lean back and accept the gift, all the while superimposing the picture of his ideal woman onto his image of Pyrena.

When she was through, Russell believed he was thoroughly in love with her.

"God, thank you."

"Your thanks and the easing of your pain will be plenty." returned Pyrena in a genuine tone.

As she wiped her hands and picked up her things, Russell was sprinting ahead, trying to find someway to keep the vision going, all the while fighting the sleepiness trying to claim him.

"Pyrena, would you like to be together this evening?" he finally managed to ask.

"That's really sweet, Rusty," she began.

"Oh God, the cop out. I'm a fool," he thought.

"… but don't mistake a substitute for the real thing."

"No, I wouldn't," he said, believing it, "but we might be pretty good together, you and I."

"Except for the black and white thing," Pyrena added.

"Except for the black and white thing." he agreed. "But that doesn't… "

"And except for the fact that we haven't spent a whole heck of a lot of time getting to know each other," she interjected.

"I think we know each other pretty well."

"AND, except for the fact that you're in a lot of confusion, maybe, over just who you are. Along with a few other exceptions, we might be King and Queen of England tomorrow." Pyrena finished.

"But I have these feelings for you. You seem to fit the bill, or rather fill out my want list." Russell pleaded, definitely feeling foolish.

"Listen, Rusty. And I would like you to get this, okay? Not every woman you meet is going to be the woman for you. That should be obvious to you by now. Not every one is going to be it."

"I realize that."

"Maybe you're just finally finding out what it is you really want in a woman – what does it for you." Pyrena explained with an unambiguous kindness, "I like what I see in you, Rusty. There's a lot of dignity and intelligence in there. And passion buried somewhere in there, too. I'm sure many of the things that you find in me, that you want *from* me, are things that you have to give yourself first."

Russell fought with the knowing that this was true. It meant such hard work to him.

"So, I need to be going, but we'll be able to talk to each other now, won't we?"

"Yes, I think I can do that now," Russell affirmed.

"No more ducking in from the window or pretending you're always in a hurry?"

"No. I'm sorry for that. It's hard for me to engage in conversations with people sometimes… when I'm not sure what to say to them."

"It's okay. Just have a restful evening. Come down for that iced coffee sometime soon." After helping her with the things she had brought, Russell watched Pyrena descend the stairs as he closed the door slowly.

~~~

Russell was sleepy. It was almost five-thirty and time for his nap. He moved heavily and with his age to his bedroom. He fell asleep immediately without pulling down the bedspread and without removing his pants. He didn't dream, his sleep was so deep.

"*Elaine*" was the thought that woke him up while it was still light.

"I was supposed to call Elaine to see if she was alright," he said out loud, looking over at the Westclock wind-up that showed eight-forty-seven p.m. "*To see if she's alright?*" The absurdity of it mostly eluded him. He wondered whether or not she was baiting him or what.

With a slowness that shocked him, Russell swung his legs around to the side of the bed, not sitting up yet, and prepared to make an attempt at standing.

After almost ten minutes, he finally made it to his chair in the living room, switching on the light and the television simultaneously. He changed channels for a few more minutes and found something about manatees on the Discovery Channel.

He dialed the number he had to go looking for in the phone book next to his chair.

"Hello? Elaine?" he asked. "It's Russell."

"Hello Russell, can you hold on a minute?"

While she was gone, Russell watched a manatee in shallow waters, nudging and rubbing against the stopped propeller of a boat.

"Okay, I'm back. It's nice to hear from you." Elaine said.

"Yes, I just thought I'd give you a ring, see how you're doing. I trust you're not in crisis." Russell said, not believing he was saying it.

"You're kidding," she said.

"Pardon?"

"I asked if you were kidding," she repeated.

"You asked me to call you tonight to check, didn't you?" he asked, feeling he was backing into some deep hole.

"Are you just fulfilling some obligation here, Russell? If you are, you can hang up anytime now," she said.

"No, Elaine, I really wanted to see… " *"What?"* he thought. *"What were you trying to see? See if you could put your foot in your mouth one more time today?"* "… if you had a good time last night. I did."

"Something is not right here, between you and I, Russell. And to tell the Godhonest truth, for me, the sex we had was empty."

"What?" he asked, not believing what he heard.

"I said the sex we had was kind of empty for me, Russell."

"Now *you're* kidding," he said. "You screamed your head off! You said this morning that you hadn't had so many orgasms in one night since you didn't know when?"

"That was true, but it was still an empty experience, emotionally," Elaine admitted.

"I thought we each knew what kind of experience we wanted from it," Russell said. "I thought we had covered all of that beforehand." Russell felt as though he had been taken.

"Well, I don't know about all that." Elaine said, "It just wasn't what I feel you had led me to believe and so I guess I'm disappointed in you. I think it's kind of cowardly to not be willing to see if we might be able to have a relationship.

"I know, Elaine, without a doubt, that I spelled out exactly what I was willing to do. I've been totally on the up and up, and now you're trashing what you claimed earlier was a nice experience. I'm disappointed in *you*." Russell knew he had not been exactly honest about his feelings, but knew that he had indeed been straight about communicating his limits.

"I still think you're being a coward." was all she could say.

"Let's give it a rest for now. Okay, Elaine? I'm really tired and not operating well enough to get into this right now.

"I'll call you if I feel like talking, don't call me. Alright?" Elaine directed.

Russell put down the phone after they said goodbye. Then he picked it up and slammed it down for the release. On the television, they were showing Russell the carcass of a manatee that had been maimed by a boat propeller – half of its face missing.

He watched for another hour, going up and down the thirty-two channels three times. Russell was still deathly tired. He felt weak from lack of food, lack of sleep, and from the lack of a moment's rest, he thought, from all of the people clamoring inside of him to be heard. This time, changing into his pajama bottoms, he pulled back the linens on his bed, sliding into it with only the sheet covering him, for it would be a warm night again.

In his sleep, Russell moved his body in jerks in correlation to the action taking place. He went down the railroad tracks to fight Mike McKnight again, the slightly retarded boy his age that kept taunting and throwing rocks at him. Russell took his brother Terry and found Mike and Mike's brother up the bank and in the field above. In his sleep, Russell's jaw tightened and relaxed, tightened and relaxed, with the words that were hurled at each other. Mike refused to leave Russell alone. Again and again he taunted Russell and refused Russell's offer at a truce. Russell continued to try to be logical with Mike.

In the end, Russell had gone up and hit Mike, demanding that Mike give in, and hit him two more times until there was blood from above Mike's eye and on Russell's knuckles. Then Russell knew he had done something bad and he backed off, his brother urging him back down the tracks and Mike McKnight screaming in rage, the veins popping out on his forehead and neck. Mike's own brother held his arms from behind to prevent him from launching the very large rock in his hands at Russell.

Later, after a period of rest, Russell reenacted the Cub Scout fight with Ricky and somehow managed to get out of sleep and out of bed to go pee, only to fall back into bed diagonally and sound asleep immediately.

Then Russell dreamt the most vivid dream. If Russell could have consciously watched it instead being part of it, he would have thought it totally void of plausibility. But he dreamt it just the same.

He came into this dream from another, less significant dream in which he had increasingly become agitated to the point of physical conflict. Again.

Contact. That's what he dreamt his few male friends would think he should have was a little contact with Elaine – of the knuckle sandwich variety. Other men he knew would agree. He thought *"God, don't start thinking about that"* because he really didn't want to think he was like them. But contact. Contact! like pushing the plunger down to dynamite the face of a hill. A small physical movement that created an electrical contact that produced a physically irretrievable result. But, geez, it would feel good. To have a little redress for all of the cheek-turning that he did because he couldn't allow himself to act the way others act. Knowing that their actions and words come from a lack of Self – they were never really directed towards him.

Russell experienced a lull in his dreaming, then found himself just about ready to abandon the path towards violence when Elaine says it – "You're too chicken" – and he snaps and then Bam! it's his hand and wrist whipping out from his arm like a backhanded racquet swing – a slapping sound contacting with the flesh on her cheek, then knuckles raking across teeth, being sliced, her head snapping back, her white neck revealed above the ivory collar and bow of her business suit, perfume hanging in the air where her head had been and his hand, not bleeding yet, suspended in the air as she brings her head back to position, the tears already forming in her eyes with total, TOTAL disbelief.

In his sleep, he turned over on his side, tangled up in his sheet and felt that all he was about was the rush of blood in his face and heart and ears. He can see that it's the same for Elaine with the addition of tears. Suddenly his brain registers thoughts again and its of *"Jesus, what have I done?"* and *"I'm sorry, I'm sorry, I'm sorry"* and of all the other thoughts that will take him back to being the wonderful, magnanimous, forgiving and repenting guy that he's always taken pride in the thought of.

These thoughts present themselves to her on his face and she says in a tone of real discovery, "You sonofabitch chickenshit!" through her tears and running makeup. And Russell hears the anger in her voice, the hate building and drowning out her knowledge of his kindness and caring and unrelenting forgiveness. He can't believe it. There is but one thought that he thinks but can't even speak aloud. And as Russell watches himself going out through the door and closing it softly, carefully, behind him, the thought continues: *"Turn the other cheek. For Christ's sake, Elaine, turn the other cheek before it's too late."*

"It's not Elaine I'm angry with, It's me." Russell knew this as soon as he opened his eyes. "I've allowed myself to be led into irrational acts and I've always blamed anyone other than myself." His voice echoed off the bedroom ceiling.

Russell turned his head over to see what time it was.

"Six- oh-nine." he registered. There were twenty-one minutes left until the half-hour mark. He felt amazingly awake and aware. His body had not responded yet, but that was usual now that he was in his later fifties. His mind was almost too clear. Thoughts flooded his brain. Ideas that had only been half formulated now had weight and mass like a wire frame model that had been filled and covered.

He showered and meditated, experiencing the rejuvenating qualities of both. Sitting there on his bed. Russell was aware of the anger inside – still there, but with both detachment and cognizance of a larger issue of transformation.

He asked himself, "What am I learning here? What has all the anger been about and what's it for? How come I am holding on to it so long and how can I get out of it?"

Russell tried to make a mental list:

"I am angry with Elaine for making me feel like crap."

"I'm angry at Ellen for not letting me give her love."

"I'm angry at Pyrena for being right."

"I'm angry at Mike McKnight and Ricky and all the others who forced me into fights."

"I'm angry with people wanting too much of me."

"I'm angry at not having any kind of decent male role model or mentor that I feel is worthy, so I'd know what behavior is expected of me right now."

"I'm angry at Valida. I'm really angry with Valida – she couldn't make the decision to marry me and screwed everything up!"

The last statement was difficult to think, but he felt much better for having made it. He also remembered his thought upon waking, still somewhat skeptical of it.

"If I am, in reality, angry with myself," Russell questioned, "why ?"

This was again, a difficult thing, and Russell could find no answer in the orange-red bricks across from his bedroom window. The air outside had cooled off considerably in the night and he pulled his sheet up around his rounding body. Pyrena had talked of some of these things and now Russell strove to reconcile his feelings with the idea that he chooses to have in his life whatever he has.

"I know why I'm angry with Elaine." he thought. "I'm angry because I let myself get into that situation when I wasn't completely right about it. There you go – I'm angry with myself." Russell then went down the list, more or less getting to the reasons for all of the anger.

"I still don't have a male mentor or role model, maybe I don't really need one. But I sure haven't done anything at all to search for one in all these years, either – angry at myself… God!" Russell was amazed at how it worked.

And Valida. He had not really given her any choice, he now knew with clarity. She had not been ready to marry him. He knew that he had not been ready, also, and had forced the issue before he had had to face his side of it. He hated to think of it as unrequited love, but she was someone the likes of whom he had not encountered again. It wasn't so much about who she was, but who she was to *him*.

"*What about Pyrena?*" he wondered, instantly remembering her words and acknowledging who she was to him. Valida had always been his standard by which to measure other women by, right or wrong, and Pyrena had just enlivened that knowledge.

"How long have I been lying to myself?" he asked. "Did it make it possible to think I was speaking the truth to others?"

Russell got up from the bed, going to the closet to get dressed. He put on a good pair of pants and chose one of his better shirts, putting his arms in it and picking up a polished pair of shoes. He closed the closet door to check himself in the mirror.

Upon seeing the exact same visage he had looked upon for years, Russell realized he was mistaken when he thought that he had been changed from simply identifying the problem. Instead, he recognized that he possessed, in fact, the *opportunity* to change, and this awareness brought to him an excitement and dread that he had not experienced for a long time. Standing there, buttoning his shirt, he realized what was missing. It was the picture of he and Valida, standing arm-in-arm, happier than he could have hoped to be again.

He got down on his hands and knees and searched the floor and found it, already gathering dust beneath his bed. Russell ardently kissed the photo, kissed Valida, and promptly began sneezing and spitting dust. Wiping his mouth, he thought, *"I need to turn the other cheek."* And to Valida's image, *"I acted irrationally and passionately... probably the last time I ever did."*

~~~

Somewhere past Pittsburgh, before the juncture of Interstate Seventy-Six and I-80, which ran straight past Chicago to Des Moines, Russell prayed to the God of the highway; the God of the aloneness of the road and of time with one's self, for the will to continue with his journey.

He philosophized on the distinctions of deliberation, and the differences between risk and *calculated* risk and how passion entered the equation. On the one hand, his endured loneliness and separation made him regret the impetuosity of his emotions and actions. *"But without them, would I have had passion?"* he wondered. *"And does the only difference between a calculated risk and bare risk lie in the more complete awareness of consequences, regardless of what they may be?"*

He wondered if, with the awareness of consequences, one might actually be able to appreciate and enjoy the risk-taking and its potential benefits better, while one was taking the risk anyway.

Billboards, wheat, corn, and passing motorists waved to him, wide-eyed and seeing long-missed sights, and Russell became at ease. And he became more of himself, the self before the loss of Valida. So much so, that he was given to writing a poem, a forgotten passion, on the back of the envelope containing his Mercedes registration.

He remembered Steven Shannon, his poetry professor in college. This was a man that had been a mentor to him! He had given much to help Russell, along with an understanding of life. *"I think I was just too young to make much use of his help,"* Russell observed. Most of all, though, he had encouraged Russell, always paving the way for Russell to improve himself.

Russell had taken Steven's courses three fall semesters in a row, before dropping out of college. *"I thought that I was well-equipped and ready, and that it was time to leave his protective wing,"* remembered Russell. *"I hope I can finally make him feel good about the effort he spent on me,"* he wished as he found a pen to begin writing with.

Russell, over the span of fifteen minutes, wrote:

I dive into the pool of souls.

Ripples spreading out on the surface.

Spreading and thinning.

Then quiet

and time.

And then

an explosion breaking the surface!

And multiple ripples,

and droplets.

And gasping for air from the sheer

exhilaration

Perplexed, Russell stopped writing and looked back and forth between the road and his poem. He asked himself, "What do I feel is happening to me?"

Twenty minutes passed. In his mind, Russell saw his answer as if already written. He then scribed out each word with a deliberation that permitted him to sanction the full meaning:

I dive into the pool of souls.

Ripples spreading out on the surface.

Spreading and thinning.

Then quiet

and time.

And then

an explosion breaking the surface!

And multiple ripples,

and droplets.

And gasping for air from the sheer

exhilaration and terrible despair.

I surface

with my own.

Russell knew that this poem was only a hope; that there were things he would have to give himself first. Maybe dare to give himself a second chance – to get it right. Just maybe he would be allowed the clichéd and classic 'Do Over'.

"Gee, would I get this spare tire removed in the deal?" Russell contemplated, taking both hands off the wheel and grabbing his stomach flab to show it to a trucker, sitting high enough to see as he passed, with Russell laughing out loud at himself.

As Russell neared Des Moines and his emotional destination, he felt an awareness of his 'want' open up, like Mr. DeSilva's azaleas, and acknowledged it fully.

"I WANT TO BE HEALED AND SEE THE TRUTH." he said aloud, adding other "wants" as they were made clear to him.

It was ten o'clock p.m. when Russell arrived in Des Moines, the lit-up golden dome of the state capitol building guiding his way to the heart of the city. Russell pulled the Mercedes into a Texaco station and used their phone book to find that Valida Winton still lived in Des Moines – at a different address than before and with only her first initial. He dialed the number that would place him in a situation with an outcome he had no preconceived expectation of. All he knew was what he wanted.

Valida answered on the second ring, her voice causing Russell's eyes to tear. She sounded shocked but curiously pleased to find him at the other end of the line and in town. Russell asked if he could come see her but easily accepted that she did not want to see him that night. She asked him to meet her at the river in Union park the next evening at eight. He told her he was sorry for everything he'd ever done and that it would be enough just to have told her so.

She thanked him and said, "There's no need to be sorry, Russell. Everything is always what we need. It was perfect for you to be impetuous. We weren't ready for each other – or anyone for that matter."

"I realize that now," Russell stated.

"I'm glad you do," she said.

"Maybe... " Russell began, but cut it off, letting things happen as they may.

"We'll have to talk tomorrow evening, Russell."

"Really, I'd like to wait, also," Russell told her. "I need to sleep on a few things tonight."

"Both of us do." she agreed.

~~~

They met the next evening. It was the Fourth of July, as Russell discovered, seeing all of the red, white, and blue flying from homes and car antennas and hearing firecrackers and bottle rockets whiz and burst all around them. They studied each other, taking in the changes in physical appearances caused by twenty-one years apart and marveling that they both thought the other had not changed at all. Russell told her all he had learned and intended to learn about himself.

Valida was as he remembered and the affect on him, his admiration for who she was, the same. He could not know what change life's events and his own actions had set in Valida. Even though he knew his changes were really only about himself, he now recognized that his actions had an impact on others – on Valida. And with the fireworks exploding in the air above, their reflections rippling in the river, Russell prayed to God that his emerging soul would not be lost again and that he might even be able, with time, to share it with others.

To be continued

WHAT RUNS THROUGH MY RIVER AT MIDNIGHT IS INDIGO

The soothsayer has said that her hair may be
wrapped around my wrists,
when the full moon's light is at its highest point in the sky.
It can be tied in a soft knot to lead me;
to stay my outbound motion;
to comfort me with its silky flowing succor.

While my heart disappears to transparency,
She dances among the reeds near the water.
I sit near the fire and She can see my heart
through the flames, yielding its contents.
The aorta and valves labor and I am powerless
to prevent her discoveries.

She chants three times my name and
the names of my ancestors,
and the river churns, rising up to her fingers
lain flat out facing downward.

Divining the water's inviolable meaning,
her eyes relax in the knowledge
as she turns to me, walks from the water and
through the middle of the fire.

She passes her downward-turned palms through
the searing flames
and stands before me, asking permission
with her eyes to place her hands.

Her request snakes through my mind like a tree root, impervious to
all in its path.
I had already renounced my resistance
in my morning prayers.

At once she grasps my wrists, and with
a fluid and potent motion,
She lifts and spins me into the flames!
Into the middle of the fire we journey, and my fear rises.
Yet I am not scorched, and I marvel at
the cooling presence surrounding me.

It is She. And She has called forth the
river diverted into the fire with us.
Standing at the bottom of the flames, below the fire place,
She molds time to her own standards,
slowing it in my eyes as well.
And I have never known a word for this eternity.

Now she wraps her hair 'round my wrists,
Binding me to her as the fire dies and the water calms.
In these late hours her Indigo River
suffuses my Being with her Divinity.
Her life flows through me – her gift to me.

It is now time to end my passivity.

THE MEXICO
OF MY FATHER'S BODY
(Rudy's Line)

When I was young, I remember my father once believed that my mother did not believe his name was Stewart. He had become obsessed with the notion that she had constructed another life for him that she believed he hid from her.

He set about to prove that he was who he was by creating a routine in his life that she could not find fault with – that she could come to count on as HIS LIFE.

In the mornings when he woke at five-forty-five, he made sure to lay in bed, curled around her on his side with his face buried into her ear. He would whisper in the absolute lightest tone that was close to breath only, that he was sorry, but he had to get up and get ready for work. It didn't matter to him whether she was awake or not. He would do this first thing every morning. Having made sure his slippers were precisely placed the night before, he swung his legs around and out of bed and into the slippers.

While I was his son, I didn't have such a high regard for my father's sensibilities toward his status with my mother and that might be why there was such tension between us and between his regard for me as his son and his regard for me as a separate entity.

~~~

When I saw your face this morning I understood what I might have looked like had I seen my father's face, unshaven, turning crimson, and not wanting to rouse my mother. There was no laughter there, no humor or even likability in your eyes seeing me and my checked-but-churning demons. I reached into the fridge for the carton of milk, raised it to drink, but instead put the container to my moist forehead, ignoring you. You told me that you no longer held your faith in who I was. And so I moved in my mind to a place that held room for only me. There, with the refrigerator light glowing around me, you left and I stood there for a long time.

It was light when I next thought of my father as me, coming to an image of me as my father and there was no smile, no time for a smile as there were no words, no sentiments, no actions I could take to bring myself back to the world that held all of the people like you that had come into my life.

~~~

When I took my late night walk, I saw two boys on one bicycle – one on the pedals, standing, and one on the seat behind him, legs trailing. I wondered what their parents thought of them being out that late. They looked to be only ten or eleven years old and they were wild-eyed. It was chilly and they had no coats. I thought to give them mine but then, I only had one and how would I get them to stop and how would I get it back?

Once, when he didn't know I was watching, I saw my father stop a boy – like the boys late at night – and take his name and phone number down. He raised his voice and I could hear him from underneath the window that I had been peeping into. He told the boy all sorts of things that he would do if he saw the boy out at night that late again. I heard him tell of things that I could not have imagined my father doing.

It put such fear into me that I could do nothing but run home, sneaking into my room and giving up the treat of Jane Diviss stepping out of the bath. Jane, wrapped in her soft pink towel to show me for my enjoyment alone, just enough of a crease between her breasts to keep me from telling my best friend, Peter. Just how might I ever be able to survive an inquiry from my father upon discovery at my late-night theater post?

I would be tangled in juniper and holly, dirty knees from crawling across the azalea beds. My father would stand upright and out away from the house and say in a normal volume, "Theodore, what the hell do you think you're doing?" And with a swat to the back of my head, he would tell me to get home. I wonder if he would stand for a moment, looking into Jane's window. Might he wish for more than my mother? More than the small paperback books in the bottom of his bottom drawer?

How might I, with magazines of my own in my bottom drawer, excuse myself for stopping these boys? How might I excuse myself for not stopping them? I was like lard in the fridge to these boys' purposeful transit. They had to move to get somewhere. I found my destination in not moving – not deciding. In not choosing. Were they as dissatisfied with their destination as I?

If I am not able to be *satisfied* with my destination, maybe the places I have been, could, at least, appease my sense of lack of destination in my life. Numbers, though, have a credibility of certainty to me. The number ten-oh-three has followed me around all of my life. I only say 1003, because it's really another number. But since I am so connected, so entangled with this number, I've been forced to use it for all of my bank account PIN numbers, my computer passwords, and have even insisted on safe deposit box and telephone numbers containing this combination.

~~~

The place that brought my awareness to this recurring number was the house at 1003 North Thirteenth, just off Vine Street in Kansas City, Missouri. I say the Missouri part because no one ever goes to Kansas City, Kansas, but everyone thinks Kansas is where Kansas City is.

1003 is – was – a two-story condemned house next to the building that was to become my business location and home in 1985. There is no one thing about this house that brings me home to 1003, the number of my life. There are many things that I remember about it, though. And I can imagine the junkies, sniffling and cold, in the boarded-up room that had been the bathroom, heating the liquid in their tarnished, blackened spoons. They were gone when we took the house. All the life and close-to-life that had been there was gone. Except for the chicken. The chicken lived in the bathroom – in the bathtub – the rim of the bathtub being its perch. I'm not sure if a chicken can be colored, or if it has to be a rooster to have color, but we called it a chicken and it was brown and red and orange and absolutely beautiful in its contrast to the smoke-darkened, water-damaged bathroom in 1003 North Thirteenth.

From that time on, 1003 has appeared on pencils, ticket stubs, serial numbers on expensive camera equipment, and I have been going through my memory boxes that I keep in the garage I found that had it's own street number of 1003.

~~~

The garage that my father ruled over in Delafield had no street address of its own, but it could have been a whole empire unto itself, the way my father had it set up, and with his rules for conduct and the operation of its features. After a rain, the hard-packed dirt floor smelled like the night crawlers my brother Randy and I would snatch up in the garden after dark and after we had watered the dirt to bring them out, our hands smelling like them and the dirt and the slime that covered them.

I could never get used to the clear, viscous covering when there were maybe fifty or sixty of them in one Folger's thirty-two-ounce coffee can. Later, out fishing, my brother would make me put my hand into the pile of them up to my small, eight-year-old wrist.

When it became late afternoon, the sun had been moving over the green, paint-chipped rowboat that we tied up to the boat wreckage just off the island. The smell of those worms seemed to stick to the can, to the bottom of the seats in the boat, and to my hands and fingers that I tried so hard to avoid wiping my nose on but couldn't.

~~~

On that day in the summer on a Sunday after the rain and after Reverend Jones had gone home, getting his fill of fishing and drinking beers with my father, I stood in the opening of the garage. The gray-painted doors were swung full open to let any kind of breeze in to counter the almost straight-on sun beating down on the asphalt shingles. My root beer Popsicle melted in between my sucks on it and while I watched my father work away on his latest project. He sang a Frank Sinatra song in his deep and sensual singing voice – a voice that made me believe he was more than just my father. I stood in the doorway in the shadow the sun made from above and behind the garage – through the breaking of my Popsicle in half; through the root beer become mostly ice at the bottom of the stick; and through the entire song my father sang underneath the fluorescent light above his cluttered worktable.

His arms were working, moving, laying imaginary paths across the tabletop. Arms like celery stalks, held together with red rubber bands top and bottom and bunched up in the middle, flexing, hard, bare, and sweating. Maybe his arms were the Mexico of my father's body – the country that was not seen underneath his thick, dark blue work shirts that were continually splattered with welding sparks, leaving mysterious holes of different sizes all around his wrists and forearms and shirt front.

~~~

I imagined my father working in Mexico City, in a factory that made radiators for Caterpillar, and a Mexican himself. He would have a large family, like the one in real life, and he would stop at the cantina in the strip mall on his way home from work. He would bring radiators that he would steal in the after-hours when he would claim to be working overtime and sell them out behind the bar in the service alley.

He would tie the money up underneath his small car, on top of the leaf springs.

My mother would always have his dinner ready when he arrived home, sober, and ready to leave work behind and enjoy his family. I would never see my father drunk. He had made a standard for himself of that, but I could smell the *cervesa* on his breath, and I knew his tequila-dried lips on my forehead. My mother never minded – he was so good-natured with us during his evenings at home – she knew he would sleep early, rise early, and be at work on time to greet his boss. She never knew about the late afternoon sales, though. She believed that his pay brought home was all that he made. And even though it was barely enough to put a dollar or two into the woven basket at church, she would not have thought to ask him if it was all he earned.

He would show me, when I became sixteen, three of the twenty-one places he hid his other money. There were three places for each of us seven children and were marked on a Mexico City street map using the letters and numbers on the edges to make the code for their exact location.

I wished this were true, standing there in the summer shade with my whole life left over after finishing that root beer Popsicle.

~~~

Sometimes when I awaken, I'm eleven years old again. Wanting to pretend that my covers and sheet are anchored into my bed and I'm pinned into it. I can lie there and listen to all of the goings-on in the house. My two feather pillows cradle my cheek and forehead and a feather quill pokes through into the skin on my jaw and I wiggle it to feel the sharpness in contrast to the soft warm flannel pillowcase. I can smell the smells of being human ground into the pillow as I swish my bare forearms and legs back and forth across the taut sheets.

I feel that if I could lay there until I grow up, there would be things waiting for me that I had dreamt of. There would be a home to return to that held me in it as the most secure of sanctuaries. There would be someone – maybe a brother – who would be there to show me how well his life had turned out and who would show our home movies on a real Daylab home movie screen. The movies would be of me, performing for the camera, showing off my athletic prowess, and always introducing my mother and father as two of Delafield's most upstanding parents and citizens.

The movies my darling brother would show, depicted me out of bed, alert, ready, moving, and anticipating each action around me. For too soon would I be back in that bed underneath my sheets, flattened, secured like a wound forming a scab underneath a very tight Band-Aid.

SPACES IN MY THINKING

Spring green against black trunks of trees, the smell of wet bark and last fall's leaves is the spring of my mind here in Northern Mississippi. There is not so much a winter, here, as there is a lack of summer; one needs to prepare for it just the same. I still feel pale from the season prior.

A shovel into soil sends spores searching for new, fertile ground, carried by the moist breeze. The city is a long way from here.

Mist covers me, covers the rosebuds. Covers the windshield of my Dodge resting against the timber at the end of the gravel with fine, Gaussian droplets. The chill is gone from my winter-white bones and I can move again, slowly. The loud *blat* from a motorcycle beats down the soundlessness of the mist as it roars past. I'm too far from the road to see it through the fine veil; my head turns toward it though, and I find I can move my body and so I do, moving to the rose bushes, gingerly squatting down to inspect.

Through the lower section of my bifocals, I see a small mayfly perched on curved, thread-thin legs. All of the insect's parts are arched. They combine in French curves and ellipses. Its furry tongue stabs at a dewdrop, drinking from it on the pale pink bud and I want to taste what it tastes. I think that the dew covering a flower so beautiful would be about the purest water one could ever sip.

I forget myself and kneel closer, dirtying the knees of my pants and almost losing my balance. I reach out and pull the pristine bud closer, disturbing the insect. It gives up its perch to me as a matter of course and flies off to another part of the plant. Almost without shame, I lightly run my tongue down the length of the rosebud. All the while I am cognizant of my memory of my first young wife and

Pool of Souls and Other Stories

the pleasure and reverence with which I touched her in the same manner.

"*To hell with shame and guilt!*" I think, as I purposefully run my tongue up and down the length of the pink beauty, remembering. The fragrance carries with it a taste imagined of the rosewater used in young Naomi's pastries made only for me to eat on the stoop out back of the kitchen in that eastern morning light I liked so well.

"Old man, what the hell are you doing?"

"I'm doing what I want. What damn business is it of yours?" I reply, as if in answer to my own conscience.

Suddenly, I am touched on the shoulder roughly and all at once I realize someone has seen me and I rush to stand up. I am startled out of my skin, it's all so much.

That's when I felt the ripping in my side; the heat and pain traveling up under my ribs into my armpit and shoulder, forcing me bolt upright and falling at the same time. I wanted to throw up. I remember seeing sideways the shovel lying next to me and the muddy brown boots of Tommy Rose and then his knees and then his hands coming to my face, turning my head up toward the sky, seeing his unshaven face all screwed up and then a wash of light and that's it.

~~~

As I lie here with my eyes closed, I can play all of it back slowly and add details that I didn't catch when it happened. I think I've been lying here a long time and I haven't particularly wanted to be a part of anything out there yet.

Although, it's too much time to think. I'm tired of thinking. I'll think myself to death, I think. There seems not enough spaces in between, where you can just sit and look at things, not thinking anything about them like they're pretty or dirty or old or big or a color I don't like.

When I first came to, there was a space where I wasn't thinking. I just laid there and watched what was going on underneath my eyelids. I guess it was just sort of imagining, but there were shapes that I manipulated into scenes and people that I found amusing to see. I dressed them funny and put funny makeup on the women. I created my long passed-on father as a Mario Andretti kind of man in a car racing outfit and had him racing around the track until I wanted to drive so I put him in the passenger seat next to me as we hit over one hundred and fifteen together. It was not fast by today's standards but it was plenty fast for us.

I found time to give myself any experience I wanted and what I discovered was that I could really get wild. I found myself chuckling quite often, lying there... where? I hadn't even bothered to wonder where the hell I was yet.

And with this thought, the rest of the world (which world?) came seeping back into me (or I into it?) and I opened one eye. Tommy Rose was sitting next to me, face still screwed up, staring at me. When I opened the other eye, I saw that it was only half of his face, the rest of it bandaged up, and I believed I had done something with that shovel. I tried to rise up toward Tommy but found all of the tubes connecting to my arms and a mask strapped to my face and I could only groan, lifting and pointing my chin toward him.

I was thinking and thinking and thinking of myself saying to Tommy that I was terribly sorry and asking him what had happened and how bad was it and that I would make it better for him if he would only tell me how. I was feeling helpless to communicate with the outside world.

Tommy recognized this and came closer to me. He began saying how sorry *he* was, that it was his fault for walking up so silently, scaring me, and his fault for being stupid on the gravel with his motorbike and asking what could he do for me and it seemed like the exact same thoughts I was thinking.

When it all came out, I knew all that had gone on and that nothing of it had anything to do with the shovel. Tommy's motorbike went down on the gravel and he came to my place for help and simply startled me.

When the doctors said I was through with the hospital part of recovering from the heart attack, someone called Tommy to come take me home. He had been using the Dodge since bringing me to the hospital and would drive me back in it. The hospital had made arrangements for a nurse at the house, so home I went.

~~~

It is later in the spring now, and most of the trees are in full leaf. There is not so much moisture in the air, but it's humid enough to smell the sour mulch from underneath the two big magnolia trees out front. Tommy's bandages are off and he drives down the driveway now and then and I was relieved to see that the scarring is not so bad as anyone thought. I see the sun glint off of his Harley-Davidson when he drives by and I know I have no desire to hop on that thing with him. Not that I could, physically.

I can't use my right leg at all anymore and, heck, it wasn't in great shape to begin with, so I've had the house fixed up to accommodate me. I had to borrow money against the house but I think, goodness, I'm not going to live to see the end of that banknote anyway.

The thing for me was the large planters I had made by a big burly fellow named Robert Buckner. He charged me an arm and my good leg for it but he did a fine job of it. I had him put them all along the inside of the porch railing and he painted them forest green so they wouldn't contrast with the foliage out beyond the porch.

I called the local nursery and they sent out this sweet young college girl and she spent enough hours out here to give me pictures in my mind I can live with a long time. The roses she transplanted onto the porch turned out to be real beauties that I can get over to in my wheelchair without too much fuss.

So I have time enough now to find spaces in all my thinking, time enough to see things and look at things that I only heard about and things I can only imagine. I've created whole cities and new inventions and even created a life beyond this one for myself.

And Mr. Buckner was kind enough to build those planters with legs so I don't have to lean too far down to my beautiful, precious, roses.

I HAVE RHINOCEROS HANDS
Addendum

I have rhinoceros hands. Veins lined with creosote. Limbs of wrought iron and the visage of Death.

Two of the happiest moments in life occurred a short while ago and now are gone. I wish they could be forgotten, but they will remain with me for a long time.

Those Angels that once thought me so endearing have left me in my sorrow and self-pity. All the daisies have been picked of their petals and are trodden upon.

An older man in white shirtsleeves and drooping mustache shuffles to me in the hallway. He tries to pass, but the hallway is too shallow. His underarms are yellowed and there are stains from comestibles on the front of his shirt. With eyes that are too shamed to look into mine, he begins to squeeze by with an indifference to that shame. He is hardened to his shame and now wears it as an overcoat to the inclement weather.

My shame is not hardened. It is like an oil used to anoint my forehead, now dripping into my eyes, down my chin and onto my chest and is no longer warm.

In times past, I have looked to another to relieve me of my shame. I have looked for acceptance in the many skills I have acquired. I have looked to smother my shame in the bosoms of women and in their moans and gratitude and attachment. No longer. But now, when I am granted some small relief from that shame for Honor gained from honest intention, the old man comes to squeeze by. His breath stains the moment with what he has eaten.

My acts are stained in browns and dull reds by the light of shame that falls on my Honor.

~~~

At times, I am stretched out horizontally between the curved walls of the well and it is all I can do to push outward with my arms and legs at forty-five-degree angles to keep from falling in. And always, I fall in.

~~~

One of those two joyous moments was during a frenzy of activity. It was devoid of shame. It was anti-shame.

Imagine this: a female child of five with a mass of curly brown hair, perched atop my shoulders, screaming for me to not swirl her around by looping my neck and shoulders because it scares her so, alternating with commands for me to not set her down – the look of a power-drunk President-of-the-World in her eyes. Add to this a girl of seven – a sweet girl who would never hurt a soul and is my sister from another lifetime – shouting at me to twirl her around and around as she hangs from my surprisingly strong forearm. A young boy of six, some neighbor's boy, caught up in this treasure the others have found in me, looking to me and silently clinging to my weaker, but still strong enough left forearm and unable to cry out his elation for fear of missing the next twirl and its gravitational pull. Another girlie of nine who knows that she has to fight to gain attention over the younger ones as she sees her youth's advantage slipping away, riding low on my back down to my hips with her arms around my waist, trying desperately to keep from slipping slowly down to the floor as I swing my arms and neck and twist in a spiral in the center of the room, taking care to not spill any of my precious, squealing cargo onto the floor or into one of the miniature dining room playsets arranged around the bedroom. I was at the center of this, once.

Gone now.

It must be of my doing, but it can't be. For if it were my doing I would be able to undo it. But it must be. But I can't. I am shut out from it. Barred from it. There is no blame for it, no fault. But because I cannot – or, refuse to – understand why, the shame grows still the more.

It is silent here without that moment. There is not the laughter to be shared and caused nor the tears to comfort. There is no bad thing happening or painful or sorrowful thing occurring. In fact, life is filled with things. But there is not the wild joy and sounds of pulsing, lived-life here, either.

The gift lays unwrapped but its contents are missing.

~~~

The other moment was the same, but inward. The silent elation of the Soul that's met another. And of the Soul that's met Itself. It was a moment of perfect reflection, of surety, of safety. Of surrender.

Somehow, the secret combination to my heart was found out. The dial turned, the tumblers clicked. A complicated sequence that has only been discovered maybe once or twice in my life. I did not try to conceal the combination this time.

I was brave. I was willing. I risked to love and be loved again. And it was beautiful for that moment! It was complete. It was the holding of hands and an arm around another, suspended in time for an hour and that was enough. It was everything and nothing at all. It was making love and being the best of friends without even trying or having to learn about the other because anything that could be known was insignificant compared to the reality of that moment. That's what was real – that feeling of Us. Not the specifics of a position or someone's past or hope or concern. All of those things change; new ones arise.

But not Love. Love is constant.

~~~

The old man in shirtsleeves brushes his bloated belly against mine as he maneuvers past. I can smell his sweat and so can he. He will glance up at me, finally, so that I can witness the swimming in his heart; the treading of water and the walk along the failing rope bridge over the crevasse of his shame.

He carries a yellowed and frayed newspaper under his arm. But it's not the racing section or sports or front page. It is the Opinion section that he carries. And every person who's not seen inside the old man's heart has written an article on the Opinion page.

I could tell him it's the wrong issue, that it's out-of-date, but his ears would not hear it. He's trained them to change the meaning of things that he hears. To distort the things that might grant him a wish and then rob him of its bounty. As he manages to pass and I'm finally able to go inside my apartment, I hear a deep, ancestral sigh come from him as he continues down the hall.

Alone in my room, the Welcome Home banner sags sadly across the doorway to my bedroom. My Soul is there to welcome me in Its melancholy way, unable to communicate Its knowledge and experience – unable to save me from myself but loving me unconditionally all the same. A tear falls from thin air to the floor.

The creosote moves slowly in my veins and the leathery covering over my heart pulses outward, a terrible reminder of those moments within which it was freed – the few brittle pieces that had been removed are now scabbed over. I set my iron limbs into a chair and I hear the sound of the old man's door closing behind him.

~~~

I'm told that this visage of Death is just a metaphor and I have the knowledge and intimate experience that along with Death, there is always Rebirth.

I'm told that the Welcome Home sign someday will hang lovingly with bright-colored letters. That there will be another joyous moment somewhere down the hallway.

I will believe these things because I always have. I believe them because of the saving grace of the Christ who died for me and because I am willing to die for Him.

In the meantime, I will continue the work I have begun on the huge mechanical beasts that will come alive when I have finished in the forge after sweating from the heat and the fire I toil over. The beasts will do my bidding, for myself and my families, because they will have been conceived of me – my Spirit and Faith and Soul – created from the essence of God. Conceived of love.

I will laugh at the Devil when I can, and shield him from my eyes with my Faith when I can't and I find my laughter is choked off at the heart.

I will do many things; accomplish great feats of skill, creativity, courage, and love.

I will also wait. For a time – only my Soul knows how long and to what end the waiting is for – for when those moments return. They are the most precious to me of all and I accept what comes with them – all of it. For it all feeds my Soul, lets me see myself as whole and shows me who I am. It all gives me the choice of how I want to Be.

~~~

I'm trying like hell to have the old man evicted. He is as stubborn as me and I vow to stare him down relentlessly every time he tries to pass me. I will launder these soiled clothes. I will go on.

The old man's time will come. He will be gone. I will be there to see it and will reap the rewards of my diligence.

SONATA IN THREE NOTCH, ALABAMA

She watched him – his face, up close – and said, through the space in the fence boards, "We need spoons."

There was a young boy walking, at the end of the fifty-foot fence just come around the corner, and when the boy trailed the stick along the boards, the sound and vibration of it beat in time to Roy's heart — short staccato beats.

Roy didn't answer her with his voice, but his eyes held hers until the boy passed them. Roy said, "You come around here tomorrow afternoon." That was all. She looked back at him, saw him run down a thought, catch it as if to roll it up in cigarette paper, and instead of smoking it, tucked it in his shirt pocket for later.

She wished he could see her pink striped dress — the way the belt circled her waist and the symmetry of the collar lapels, wide and flat and an invitation to the smooth-freckled skin of her throat. She swayed a little to give him more to see in the space between the boards.

He turned his body from her to leave, but left his eyes with her and she saw his eyes the rest of the day; when she lay down at night with her mother in the big bed and all the way through her dreams of carnivals and baby carriages and the butchering of animals. And in the morning, when she woke, when she rose and looked in the mirror to see what was left of herself, she saw in place of her own, the innocent, burning, loving-cruel eyes of Roy's.

~~~

Standing there at the fence for so long, waiting, she had an old deja vu – a dream deja vu – that reminded her of the woman at the Whiteway drugstore. The woman waited on the fountain customers in her pale green and white uniform. She had made the dozens of milkshake glasses spotless and had lined them up along the back counter. Their fluted, flower-like tops were turned down, like flags at half-mast, as she waited for the burial of her last customer and the corpse-dead silence that immediately followed the cheery tinkle of the small silver bells on the door.

The waiting was made all the longer by the rows of ready glasses, their numbers doubled by their reflection in the back, counter-length mirror, and by the discovered chocolate smear on the back of the woman's dress, revealed to that last, forgotten customer.

Through the small lit space between the fence boards, Roy saw her thin, pink lips touch the back of her hand. Roy allowed himself the thought that she held her hand to her lips like he thought a poem would sound, if he could have remembered one. He could have lived there in the space between the boards – in her wrist that carried the message of her lips and the essence of her soul. But he chose instead to light another cigarette. He was silent until she turned toward the fence to look for him.

"Roy!" she whispered loudly, her mouth leaving her hand. Roy would remember the wetness of saliva left on her hand for the first year and a half of his time in Fallridge Penitentiary.

She put her hand through the opening between the boards, the largest opening they had found in the fence that ran between the back of Three Notch High School and Suggs' Salvage where Roy had found a big Oldsmobile station wagon to sleep in.

Roy looked around, then pulled his right hand from his back pocket and grasped her small, smooth, and unpainted fingers, looking for the back of her hand and wishing she wore lipstick, imagining a trace of it transferred from her lips. It would have been a landing zone for his own lips, but he reached down with his mouth anyway, to taste the wetness from her mouth; to sip, to savor, what he would rather have gulped down until he was dead from drowning and until she was dead from the loss of life given to him.

He stayed that way, with his head bowed down, licking, kissing, sucking up into him as much of her as the small space in the fence of fifty feet and eighty-nine boards would grant him as pardon for crimes against her, and therefore, against society.

He could feel her body talk to him, through her hand and wrist; her body moaning for clemency, for early release from the wait, from the nights lying next to her mother in the big but not big enough bed, and he became angry at her. Not angry in a way that would make him stop loving her, but angry in a way that would urge him to continue loving her, as punishment.

Still with lips touching her hand, Roy looked up the length of her arm, raising it slightly to see up into the puffed sleeve of her dress and to her shaved and smooth armpit, a bit of the round cup of her brassiere, and he saw drops of her sweat run down her soft skin to along the curve of the fabric, wetting it, darkening it. It was two feet and three hundred miles from where he could get to, and he burned with the anger.

"Dear God, we need spoons," she moaned.

"We won't need spoons just as soon as I get the Ford rolling," Roy told her.

"When, Roy?" she asked, tilting her head to the side to see through the opening.

"Tomorrow."

"Tomorrow?"

"Yeah, tomorrow. I just need to get a damn battery," Roy said.

"Tomorrow? That soon? Really, Roy?"

"All these junks got no batteries that are any good," Roy told the junkyard behind him. He didn't see the panic in her eyes. He only looked for the one vehicle he might have missed that might hold their — his — salvation.

She saw in her mind for the first time since speaking of leaving with Roy, the actualities of their leaving. Of what she would have to do. She didn't notice Roy letting go of her hand as she saw herself telling her mother what she had planned, telling her that she would be gone, that she would not be sleeping in that big bed; and seeing the way her mother would stay away from that side of the bed, never even turning over toward it but looking out away from that side with her eyes open, red and tearing, through every night until when... she could not imagine. How would she say the words to her mother?

She knew she would be able to finish packing. She knew she could step into Roy's Ford, slide along the vinyl seat until her hip found his, not look back or even into the rear-view mirror; but she was terrified that her words would turn into sobs — into unintelligible croaks, standing before her mother's death.

"Tomorrow," Roy commanded her. "Anytime after you've had your last lunch with your mother." He turned from her first, as usual, paying attention to the long ash on his cigarette and never seeing what she held for him in the trembling of her lips, the redness of her eyelids, and the closing of her shoulders as she pulled back her hand.

She saw everything.

~~~

Tomorrow. Did not come. At least, the tomorrow she had imagined, did not come.

Roy left her with the anger that had come to him, along with his kiss left to etch his claim on her. She had walked away in her little black flats and her girlish, straight-legged schoolgirl gait, her blood drained and her emotional body floating out somewhere too near the power lines looking for either a source of energy or an electrocution.

In the morning, with her light brown hair turned dark wet, the summer of her last year on earth as a girl female, she sat with a breakfast of grits, over-easy eggs, and toast in front of her made by a mother who knew everything about her, knew nothing about her she didn't want to know. Her mother gone-to-work-til-lunch-come-back that had always been there in that apartment subsidized by the state.

The eggs were gone hard and the butter had unmelted on the toast as she read the front page article over and over five or six times until she had put each sentence after the other until it made sense to her. What she always knew would be true had been found out by almost everyone before her: Roy had been a bad thing. Not so bad as he could have, but bad enough to throw her mind into a whirlpool of thoughts smudged into a spiral that traveled down into her belly with nowhere else to go.

Roy had been caught stealing a battery from a car in the new residential section of town by a policeman living across the street. He had handcuffed Roy and taken him inside his home. And while the rest of Three Notch was still held back in the fifties, the officer who lived on this newly concrete-and-curbed street had a computer in his house, knew how to use it, and had contacted the state-wide criminal referencing center to discover that Roy was wanted by warrant for the severe beating of a young girl he had planned to marry.

The newspaper article told of the violent and sad past that Roy had brought with him to Three Notch; the past that she lived in his kisses that forced their way into her mouth and heart and dreams; the past that she could feel but not put to knowledge.

~~~

She stood when her mother came through the door at the lunchtime that was to be their last together. Her mother smiled at her, brought the bag of groceries to the gray Formica kitchen counter, and put them away, each item in its usual place.

"I see there's a suitcase there by the bed," she said, opening the upper cabinet that held the dry goods. "Can you talk to me about this?" she asked.

"Yes."

"Good. Well, sit down and we'll talk. Alright?"

She sat down in the chair that blocked her mother's view of the suitcase and watched her mother in her pale green and white uniform, moving like a normal person, until they were both sitting, her mother's forearms laying flat on the surface with her hands together and her thumbs rubbing one another.

Her mother and she looked directly into each other's eyes as they had always been able to do.

Her mother asked, "Are you alright?"

"I know I *will* be," she answered.

Her mother said, "Good. Before we talk, I want you to know that I heard about the Roy fellow you've been seeing and I've had all sorts of thoughts about how all of this... all of us might turn out − all the possibilities." Her mother looked into the girl's eyes for confirmation of any of these and went on: "Are you planning to leave still? Or did you make up your suitcase after you read about him?"

"I was planning to leave with him, Mama, but I did make up my suitcase anyway, after I heard."

Her mother caught a breath, almost like a hiccup, and straightened in her chair. She said, "I've been seeing the dreams you have. I never wanted to intrude in them, but at night in that big bed, I've seen your dreams where you go roaming. They come to me like my own, but when I saw myself in them, and Roy, I knew they were yours."

"Mama."

"I love you, Margaret Ann, and I will try to protect you from a bad fate, if I can. Some of those dreams scared the stuffing out of me, so I've been getting ready."

"Mama, I love you, too. I don't want you to be hurt by me." she said, seeing the tears that formed in her mother's blue eyes and blurred by her own. Her mother took the girl's hands in hers across the table.

"So don't go right now," her mother continued, "and we'll work out a plan for you. A plan that can keep you safe and out of the trouble that I've seen in your dreams. I can't keep you from where you're going, but I can help make sure you get there and not somewhere else by anyone's bad hand."

Margaret Ann wept, sitting in her chair with her mother holding her hands, and knew that she would be able to stay for a while, in the big bed with her Mama, who had her dreams.

~~~

STAIRCASE

It was a moment that was rolled around a short corner, dropping for what seemed like a whole afternoon at a nightmare dentist's; dropping down into the bottom of my esophagus and choking off what might have saved me.

Its surprise, a long-winded cyclone hurrying me to what would be the antithesis of her splendor, and my wait, made all the more horrible by the fingerprint of her scent; the non-sound in the banister wood; and that one small navy blue pump left at such an angle as to have been unnoticed by her achingly beautiful and indifferent foot as she was carried up the stairs by someone other than myself. I could hear their laughter.

What might have saved me would have been to turn around and leave in the midst of that rolling moment. To have given up all love for all time in ignorance; to stand out in any downpour; to grasp the lightning rod and burn all knowledge of that moment from my cells and bloodstream and lineage.

By what means or perseverance of muscle was I to lift my leg to move off of that next stair? My shoe was muddy. I could trace where the mud had come from, what it contained in it. But could I predict its path – my path? Who could tell me? There was no one to tell my fortune and I wanted someone to lie to me like I needed in that moment to end my breathlessness.

Funny, I had come to her door with the wanting to land small airplanes on her small white torso as I recited the most joyfully memorable moments from my childhood. I would launch my toy battleships from between her breasts, telling her of my boyhood battles – the battles in which I won – and call her "Tora" the whole evening.

In that spinning moment, I could have been a weapon myself. I could have been a white-hot-metaled ship's turret blowing a hole through her house, one fifty-pound shell of pain and anger at a time, randomly, stopping the guns of my hate only when the bed where she floated with this... man – this enemy – was blown out from under them.

To have been such a child, allowing the hope of joy, the thrill of laughter – actually imagining playing with toys on her naked body! It was, now, such an amazingly absurd image that I thought I might heave, thereby chancing my discovery.

My mind went out in search of sanity. It left my body and wandered along the beamed ceiling and rolled over, dipped, and It became afraid of not finding Its way home. I reached out to grasp It, asking It, pleading It to... my mind broke into a wide, wide grin, like a sharp-toothed cartoon wolf, looking at me and asking, "Well, what would you like to do now?"

My mind went ahead and launched its own battleship – a hulking, powerfully-engined metal wedge with which to split my opposing mental paths.

One path led to surrender and I could imagine myself disembodied, my small self forever cut off from any sense of larger

Self – a psyche without a home – without any means of fulfilling its puny desires. The other path led to rage, disgust, hatred, action, and the slim, fine-haired possibility of either satisfaction or oblivion.

I climbed the stairs walking the line between the two, one mind snarling blood-wet-lipped carnivorous exclamations at the other mind that was cowering, peeing its pants in the tight, ninety-degree corners of each stair riser.

I thought for a brief moment to give the cowering mind power. To imagine an outcome derived from giving an advantage in strength of conviction to the little guy. It smiled cautiously, looking back down the stairs. I asked it what it would do with the advantage. Would it take me out the door, never to return to the woman's place again? Never to call her? To remove her things from my closet, from the kitchen, and from my bedroom dresser? Would it create a scenario that ignored what the whole mind had seen and what that other mind had imagined it would do if given the opportunity? Would it dare, ever, to allow love in again at all?

This less powerful mind allowed my eyes to look downward, at the fifth stair of the carpeted staircase, to see that it was threadbare, corresponding to the part of her that held its esteem for me and I wanted to kneel before her, if for nothing else, to cover up the ruined areas of her love for me – to shield her from her knowingness of it.

And as it looked down, the small mind's diesel-driven twin swung back its splayed-out and gleaming scythe to end the whimpering, end the tale about to be told by the weaker mind. I turned upward toward the heavens waiting to be split apart at the top of the stairs.

My shoes – my muddied loafers with neatly pre-tied tassels – became the largest and thickest of almost-black, steel-toed, steel-everything motorcycle boots.

Now, as I hear the CLUMP of one of my boots stepping onto the hallway floor, the mind that splintered the banister with its gnawing, bloats to fill the hallway, consuming the laughter and voices coming from behind her closed bedroom door. It thinks, "Heeeeere's Johnny!" as I witness my hand grasp the doorknob, believing it could rip the door from its hinges like a bizarro Superman – the anti-Superman.

As the door pushes open easily, it's as though my evil Superman's cape were tangling itself about my neck, choking me – my demon mind running out of its stuff as my eyes see her figure, alone, propped up in bed and a spoonful of melting ice cream halfway to her mouth with her head pointed towards the television but her eyes turned toward me.

"Hey, hi!" she says and I'm lost at sea, the divided minds running for cover, sucking themselves back into my brain casement to leave me with all of their litter coursing through my body like I've swallowed an electric eel whole and alive.

My mouth moves and asks her what's on TV and I become a puppet to some other being that pities me, allowing me to sit and act out the rest of the evening as a human being. It does a good job. I just might make it through this night.

MY CIGAR ANGELS

I don't want anyone to say that I've suffered. If I were to see it in print I would be livid. To suffer. What an idea and what images it brings to mind.

I want no part of it.

I have lived with God at my feet and in my heart and with Angels at each elbow as if I were an old crotchety man being lovingly helped down the hard-as-nails steps in the old courthouse.

I have smoked cigars with the Angels.

That is to say that I have been with Angels and while in their company, have smoked a cigar. Angels would never smoke a cigar.

To create an image of them in my mind doing so just doesn't work. How could they bring themselves to lift the brown cylinder to their mouths? Brown! They would never have brown things in their hands – even the brown Angels. I could see them grasping gold objects, lighter-than-pastel objects, and at Christmas time, maybe a few red and green items.

And to imagine them putting a cigar to their faint-thin lips, wetting it, wrapping it with their Untouched tongues? Forget it!

What they'll never know! is how I think of it.

With the Angels at my side, I have taken that smooth/rough fellow, cradled and anchored in the niche of my hooped-around index finger, and merely contemplated the smoking of it as I lovingly clip the little bud-end. A ritual. A circumcision. The Angels stand by, curious. They wait for my indulgence. I put them off by waiting myself, and search for a classic and full-bodied joke to tell them while I wait. The Angels will laugh, if I tell it correctly – something that is always possible when I am waving a cigar around in my hand, lit or not.

They like to study me, I think.

When I am in cigar-waving mode, I am unpredictable. I am in my own top-form territory, my own sovereign dominion, and while they never speak to me directly, I can tell. It makes them nervous. I will waddle around, turning suddenly to the left with a twist of my body and the raising and tilt-back of my head and left shoulder to see who has come by; see who has spoken words that I might have some grand and shrewd come-back for. It could be the President of the United States – even a Democrat – come up behind me with an Eh-hem! from the Secretary of State and I would raise my eyebrows, cigar poised in the air to the right of my right shoulder and swing around to see who it was that might need some quick-witted barb to loosen their tie knot.

In situations like this, the Angels move behind me, so as not to be seen. As if they could! They stand close together, one's leg and whole side dipping into the other's. When I look back at them, they try to look composed. Two Angel bodies almost as one standing there would not necessarily be any big deal. It's the fluttering. The little nervous fluttering of their wings catches my eye and when they see my eyes watching their wings, POOF!, they're gone. Chickens.

That's when I will deign to light up. It draws them back. Any sort of fire or smoke will do that. I believe they figure it's either an emergency or some ceremony and don't want to miss either. It's kind of an obsession with them.

By the time they come back, I've had the taste. And they are ever watchful for who may be in my vicinity; who may be tempted to engage with me during my smoke.

But in the first part of the smoke I am not a threat. I am too involved with my Macanudo to notice much other than the twirl of the leaf against my lip; it darkening, releasing the flavor of this fruit of rich earth – an opening curtain to the opera of aromatic dance that is to follow.

Wait. Wait 'til I bring out the Bulldog.

Trading off the cigar to my left hand, a mirror of the right's protective tenure, I slip – operative word: slip – my right hand straight down into my pocket. Straight down to the bottom, weighted down by the Bulldog, and grasp the metal thing, bringing him out, to show anyone, the final answer to a Man's Lighter.

The Bulldog is the most stocky, tank-of-a-cigarette-lighter you'll ever come across. Its stainless steel case is worn smooth and shiny, but the big Mack Truck insignia is as distinctive as ever and I always marvel at how well it has held up.

It came to me across a heaping, starch-heaven plate of steaming mashed potatoes, gravy, stuffing, and sliced turkey in North Platte, Nebraska. Literally. Evelyn the waitress passed it to me from the other side of the U-shaped counter in the Pull-R-Inn truck stop out on I-Eighty. It belonged to Alvin T. Bourdois, pronounced Bor-dwah, from Oberville, Ohio. Twenty-one-eighteen North Lilac Street. One, four-two-two, six-three-eight, one-oh-one-oh. I know because it's engraved on the other side of the Bulldog, although it's getting harder to read.

Alvin had been complaining about his CB radio quitting on him and how expensive they were in the truck stop store. I had pity on him after the other fellows at the counter ribbed him to no end, asking him if he wanted any cheese with his whine, and I asked him what he had to trade for a CB. He pulled the Bulldog out, held it up in the air for all to see with an explanation of what exactly it was, and our counter and two counters over became dead-quiet.

This scared me. I blurted out, before another word was said, that I had a CB and he could have it for the lighter. Well, all eyes turned from the lighter to me, and Alvin shouted out SOLD! before anyone could say anything.

Evelyn the waitress passed it over to me and I told Alvin I would go out right then to get my CB and all the wiring and left my plate of food. I walked over to the trucker's store, bought the cheapest CB radio they had, took it out of the box, tossed the box and wrapping and twisty-ties into the trash, and headed back to the restaurant to give it to Alvin. I left that truck stop in Nebraska with the Bulldog.

I've never regretted it. It lights every time.

As it lights up, I bring it to its duty, the Bulldog ready to burn the house down if it must. I grab hold of the cigar with a baby's touch of teeth and my lips like a smooch and I draw in.

With several quick draws, the harvest of Connecticut rolls into my mouth, just as it spirals into the air in front of me. And the woods and valleys of the better part of a tropical country clot my tongue, fill my veins with a remembrance of living as I rarely have known it. I am at peace and at home and anyone that comes to me here had better mind themselves.

POOF! The Angels are back to see what's on fire. Every single time they are surprised to see it's just me with a cigar. They seem to have no memory or expectation that they take with them from moment to moment – something I have been wise enough to begin learning from them.

I nod to them, bid them welcome back, stick my cigar into the cul-de-sac at the end of my mouth, and shove both hands into my pockets along with the Bulldog. The Angels know what's next as I begin to rock on the balls and heels of my feet, looking for trouble, and their wings begin to flutter.

No. I have not suffered so long as I have had my cigar with God at my feet and in my heart and Angels at my side.

THE SUN WORSHIPPER

I believe that am at my best when the sun moves through the sky from morning until dusk, and even a short time after.

Before that, the uncertainty of what the day may hold brings me coffee getting cold and sleep in my eyes. I resist life. Birds can call out to me in lilting melody only for me to perceive it as a raucous and invasive taunting. Before the sun has filled the window sill, this could be a day I die or hurt someone or produce nothing of value and worth.

I am anxious for the sun to enter my life and restless with the inability to cause anything. Without a result on record for the day until this minute, how am I to gauge and measure what the beating of my heart has been meant for?

Should I take some solid object and crash it into another? I imagine a gigantic oriental gong, as big as a car and shining golden in the morning shadows. I would lift a massive mallet, swing back with it, threatening the dislocation of my shoulder, and launch it into the meat of the metal, off center. The impact would cause my teeth to clatter and my arms to bounce back, almost losing my grip on the mallet.

But the resulting kinetic shock and swell in the massive tam-tam would consume the air surrounding me and send a signal to my ears and Nature to get the hell out of the way because the sun is coming, rays of it streaking in onto the hanging brass disc still returning from its trajectory outward.

I have been standing, incoherent except for this vision and just long enough for the sun to finally seep into our small living room above the mighty Chaophraya River, eight stories down and at the eastern back of our building here in the Khlong San river district of Bangkok.

The sun's rays of light are life-giving to me. That's what I've chosen to believe and it's what I keep telling myself until I now both live by it and am bound to it.

Now I can react to my wife with civility and love and move toward the plans that I purported to construct during my time before sundown yesterday. Am I a reverse Dracula? A Bizarro Vampire that can only thrive during daylight, retreating to my mental coffin as night descends? How silly I've become.

It's all a fantasy and only my perception in these moments so far today.

Normally, I'm a go-getter and switched "ON" upon waking. And that's what's actually annoying to my good wife. Because she's the one with Morning Reticence Syndrome.

~~~

As the early morning Saphan-Taksin Ferry leaves the pier with its gray-blue diesel smoke filling the air, two things are on my mind.

One is that I love being on the water. It doesn't matter that the Mighty Chaophraya is dirty and churning from the dozens and dozens of boats that travel the few Bangkok-dividing miles.

The tugs leading barge caravans carrying sand and rice up and down the river to the many high-rise construction sites and markets, respectively, are quickly passed by the open and ornate boutique-style passenger boats comporting the wealthy guests of luxury hotels and condominiums.

The shore-to-shore ferries like the one I'm on must defer to the hotel and dinner cruise boats, angling to break their wakes at forty-five to ninety degree angles to avoid capsizing during the river rush hours. We're taking commuters across the river to the more modern and built up "downtown" of the city.

I'm headed to find a thirty-Baht breakfast of rice, pork, basil, and fried egg. Thirty Baht is the equivalent of about ninety-five cents, USD.

That it's worth it to spend five Baht each way on the ferry in addition to the kra-pow breakfast speaks to the necessity of being spendthrift as my wife and I try to manage living on just her salary. That I later plan to break our agreement and spontaneously spend another forty Baht on the Bangkok Transit System train to venture further into the city and further away from the water will become the catalyst for the anvil-drop into calamity to follow.

But for now, being seated in the ferry at almost water-level, I can imagine I am *in* the water. The waves and wakes of other boats come right up to me. I could touch a seal or large bullhead if it surfaced next to where I am in the wide, flat-bottomed water bus. Unmoored bright green water lilies, the kelp of the Chaophraya, come alongside the boat and give a freshness to the brown-gray color of the water.

The rooster tail plumes of spray trailing extended propeller shafts of the long-tail boats sparkle with silver effervescence in the morning air for us. The long-tails' massive v-eight car motors roar like the Daytona Speedway and I want to know about these Evel Knievels, these NASCAR stock car drivers of the water.

I watch as one driver puts to bear all of his dark-muscled weight onto the steering shaft, straining to get the multi-colored rocket to back up toward another dock. I imagine these guys are really no different than someone like Big Daddy Don Garlits, strapped in just ahead of a 1000 horsepower, nitro-burning, slingshot dragster. These river racers do it with no helmet, no flame-proof suit and mask – just a huge raw engine mounted behind them, a pole in their hands to steer and a longer, propeller-ended pole in the water, hurtling along the choppy artery that flows to the Gulf of Thailand.

As he gets his craft turned, sunlight floods into the boat and the sweat glistens along his knotted forearms and face turned outward, illuminated like a gladiator surveying the crowd in a hot and dusty arena, looking for a patron. But I think I might just tend to romanticize these taciturn Thai river men a bit.

The Second Thing on my mind as the ferry chugs across the waterway is a desire to see the area of Bangkok where all of the prostitution goes on. That's a shocking admonition.

I kind of believe they don't even exist and while my wife has given me so many examples and warnings of the ways these women – and often women who are men – come on to foreigners, entrap them, I have seen not a trace of this kind of activity in the area where we live.

"These women will compliment on your eyes, your height, your body – even if you were more fat-bellied than you are," she says.

I say, "But you know I am not at all interested in that type of thing."

"It does not matter. They will use anything they can get you to come along with them. They even appear very innocent and like dolls and they know all tricks to make men want to go with them."

"But I am not like other men. You know that. It's too much trouble to get into that kind of thing. It's never worth it," I protest.

She looks at me sideways, that knowing Thai-woman-look. "Just stay away from them. That's all."

I don't even know where they are in the city. But if wanted to see where they are, I imagined I would go looking during the day, just to be safe. After all, I'm invincible during the day, during sunlight hours. I could just go and check the scene out a bit.

What would be the worst thing to happen? And how could I later include this subject of the seedy side of Bangkok in stories I might tell with any amount of veracity if I have only cautionary anecdotes from my wife? What weight would that carry in a circle of cigar-chomping and Chang Beer-drinking friends? If I had any of those.

But as the ferry sideswipes the old tires that roughly cushion the floating dock from the half-hourly onslaught all day and evening, the bounce jars me from those thoughts and reminds me I'm on a tight budget; on my wife's tight leash as well. I hop off with the others, forcing those waiting to board to wait just four seconds longer before pushing each other onto the ferry.

I can't put it all on my wife. I have very strict standards for myself as well regarding our marriage and I have no desire to put myself at risk of that kind. Whenever I even try to imagine myself "straying from the marriage bed", the single word, "Trouble", with a capital T, is immediately on the tip of my tongue.

I've never transgressed in that way. Not even through my three previous marriages, the latter two of which were less than, let's say, agreeable.

And while I will take credit for staying both emotionally and physically faithful, the truth is that during those rough times, it was easy, because I imagined that every attractive woman that I might bounce my eyes from was Trouble. Even the ones that might seem they might be nicer to me, I projected that they would eventually become mean and ugly. I recommend this technique to any married guy. Maybe the single ones, too.

Ah, is that a misogynistic streak in me?

After disembarking from the ferry, I walk beneath the three-legged Taksin Bridge, named for the king whose name I have to research. I am called to by the many Tuk Tuk drivers, minimal street food vendors, long-tail boat cruise schedulers and the many other enterprising sellers of *whatever* who've set up shop along the Soi leading to the Main Street on this side of the Chaophrya.

The sun is already making its mark on yesterday evening's pavement leftovers and workers who must wear conventional office attire made of skin-suffocating polyester and patent leather. It generally ripens the fruit of Bangkok's day.

I am quite fortunate. My fortune allows me to wear light shorts similar to swim trunks; a thin, short sleeve, light blue-striped button up shirt open to my chest; and open hiking sandals. It is this, in part, that affords me the luxury of claiming to love the sun and the heat. Of course, if you're able to wear next to nothing, have no one to see and nowhere to be and so can sweat your way through the day, what's to complain about?

I pass by the woman quickly selling out of her clear plastic containers of white rice, a mystery pork and gravy, and a fried egg atop it all. I know from experience that she is the wife or partner or something of the guy up at the corner who hawks their main supply of thin, clear, BPA-infused food containers, and I will go to him to buy.

For some reason, I rationalize that because his station is the source of the little meals, it is probably more safe to eat from there. Like it must be more fresh or hot or... In truth, he doesn't even cook it there, unlike other street vendors, and so it should be even more suspect in my mind. But since coming to Bangkok, I find I rationalize many things with irrational thinking.

My thoughts are occupied by these types of self-conversations much of my time here in the city that makes Los Angeles look like a hamlet.

Should I rinse my mouth out after brushing my teeth and spitting into the sink? If I do, am I inviting bad germs from the city water system to be deposited inside my mouth to find a way into my body and make me have diarrhea for days? But then, is using that same tap water to wet my toothbrush equally endangering? If I see flies landing on an outdoor vendor's food, and I don't see them on another's, does that ensure no flies have been on that food?

I'm in a city of frequent sun. You'd think I would want to stay here...

In truth, because my wife is a Thai national and can translate for me, negotiate for me, and in general, protect me from my cultural and linguistic ignorance, I have no reason for the kind of concerns I voice. Although, she reminds me that she is from Chiang Mai, twelve hours north by car, and is not familiar with the peculiarities of a city such as Bangkok – a city which may have no similar counterpart in the world.

And in a further outburst of truth, I know I'm not really going to go looking for the red light district over on this side. I've already seen where it is, I think, by the bar names and the Hooters that seems to be center stage for who and what comes out at night.

Instead, I'll just go to McDonalds and get a McMuffin and hop the ferry back over the river and go about my day in the relative peace of the Soi 17 neighborhood. *It ain't Bangkok* over on our side and I'm glad. I could actually stay in Thailand for an extended time.

I've gone back into the apartment now and I still have the reluctance that comes up whenever I leave the sunshine. It's left over from my growing up in the Midwest where days of sunshine were at a premium. You didn't waste them being inside if your could help it.

But here? It's the tropics, what can I say? If it gets cloudy or rains, it's gone within a few hours.

My sunny disposition will return with its source.

THE ASCENSION
OF RAUL MARTINEZ

Small dark hands wring blood from a white worn handkerchief now stained red. Tears drop into the mix as he almost blindly looks to the outer door, expecting it to burst its hinges, the wood splintering from the force of Justice come to claim him. Through his tears, the tulip wall lamps create the illusion of streaming shafts of light as if angels fill his vision. He believes this is so.

Raul Martinez looks to his wife sprawled on the floor and feels she should not be seen this way – one leg twisted up underneath her from the fall and her dress half off. In the moments he has before they are lost to each other, he kneels to her, setting the once-white cloth down in the growing pool of blood, and gently brings her leg down to the other. He avoids her eyes as he straightens her dress and culpably notes the time on the wall clock.

In a breathless rasp, Alicia Martinez whispers his name. He looks to her and is greeted by the countenance of Life Everlasting. She is the crucified Jesus; the lamb at slaughter; the Madonna, the Virgin, the Hope of Mankind with the left rear of her skull collapsed. Raul Martinez reverently places his wife's folded hands over her heart with his own and kneels, praying to her – oblivious to the pounding on the outside door of the small brownstone apartment tucked away on the lower east side.

His pants knees soak up Alicia's life as the outer door explodes inward. Alicia parts her lips in an enraptured smile, at once absolving Raul of all past, present, and future.

The police stream out of the apartment, some glancing in through the window of the next apartment where a man watches them exit on the six o'clock news in black and white.

As the man reflexively cleans under his fingernails, a close-up is shown of the large brass crucifix being put into the plastic evidence bag, smearing the clear sides with blood. A slack-faced Raul Martinez is led handcuffed down the steps where he once knelt before his wife, singing the Mexican song his father had sung to his mother as she sat on the stoop, his head in her lap and she stroking his black hair.

There is no one to translate for Raul as the detectives attempt their mock Spanish, gesturing like monkeys in the fluorescent-lit, yellow-walled room. One detective – a brusque man of Greek tracings – takes Raul's silence as an affront and paces the floor, castigating him. Raul turns to peer calmly over the edge of the table and the man looks in succession down at the speckled twelve-inch square linoleum tiles beneath his feet.

Observing the worn tread in the tiles that Raul has led him to, he looks back up at Raul in terror and says, "Te amo mucho, me amor." The Greek's face turns ashen and he mumbles an excuse to the other detective, rushing out without another word. Raul's vacant stare shifts into slight contentment for a passing moment as he whispers in Spanish, "I love you, too."

The other detective, unsettled by his partner's departure, rises slightly from his chair to bring it forward toward Raul. He picks up the pen from the table and shoves it violently at Raul, commanding him to sign. Raul complies, signing his name to the confession with a minimum of hand movements, laying the pen down quietly to then look up at the man across the table from him.

The man's focus narrows as he looks into Raul's vitreous eyes, considering what it might take for a mind to justify the extinguishing of another's life. His discovery is reflected in Raul's eyes and he rises up, pulling his balled fist back to strike Raul. He stops, and speaks to Raul instead. The words lilt across the room with no echo, "Este no Silencio, no... " *("There is no Silence, no sounds that are not meant for God's ears, and the words that you and I now hear are only the calming waters singing to us from our family's fountain. It nourishes us with its bountiful flow.")*

Raul replies, "Si, ... " *("Yes, I understand.")*, as the detective snatches up the pen and paper like a greedy Baron collecting his tax from a peasant, leaving Raul to sit in the room for another six hours by himself, save for one bathroom walk.

Throughout the trial of Raul Martinez, the press characterizes Raul as "detached" and "Godless". After the verdict is read, the presiding Judge delivers his ruling, ready to condemn the man who has been reckoned to have murdered his own beloved. He asks Raul if there is anything to be said on his behalf. The public defender manages a few words in Spanish but Raul is motionless and unresponsive as he stands before the court until the Judge rises, outraged, his robes fluttering, to shake a finger at Raul and speak.

"Raul Martinez," he begins, "Este no separacion… " (*"There is no separation between you and I. No judgment exists that can be levied on you now. You are beyond that. When you and I meet again in ethereal presence, you will shed no more tears for this tragedy."*) Raul smiles as he gazes at the Judge lovingly. Raul's court-appointed attorney turns to him with suspicion when the Judge abruptly stops, weariness and anger turning his eyes to the rinds of blood oranges, his gavel fracturing the pedestal with the force of his adjudication.

Much later, after Raul Martinez is led from the metal bed he has used as his prayer altar and down through the prison's corridors in el Procession de Muerte to the gas chamber, the Jailer secures Raul for his ending. As he closes the door, the man hesitates, turning to Raul to whisper, "Nosotros… " (*"We are as One, you and I"*). The door is sealed and the gas pellets drop, but there is no one in the chamber to breathe in the fumes.

RIDING SHOTGUN

When we hit the rise just before the railroad tracks, she must've been doing about fifty miles an hour in a twenty-five mph zone, somewhere near the Overton Park Zoo in Memphis. We were airborne over the tracks.

Sometime between the time I was three and forty-three, my mother acquired a need for speed.

Now she drove Great Aunt Grace's late model American car after Aunt Grace fell and broke her hip. The car had less than four thousand miles on it after four years but it was seeing some real action on the streets these days. Aunt Grace had recently passed at the age of ninety-nine, another in the long line of old-aged southern belles on my mother's side.

Thank God Mom had both hands on the wheel when we came down with the shocks bottoming out on the other side of the tracks. My hands were white-knuckled around the armrest and holding onto the dash long after she let go of the wheel with her cigarette hand to flail it in the air descriptively as she goes off on another tangent. Heading over to Walgreen's just off of Stonewall, she was again telling me of how we would always pass Elvis Presley on our street coming home as he was headed out to Graceland while building it. Aunt Grace used to tease that he later named it after her because of how well she treated him at Union Planters Bank. And she claimed that he would always ask her to lunch but she would refuse, being that she was a professional at the bank and all.

Back then, the big two-tone green Plymouth DeSoto that Mom drove gave me no worries as she drove purposefully down streets lined with brick houses and magnolia trees. The metal visor above the windshield shaded my eyes from the southern sun as Mom sang the tunes she used to tap dance to. Add a gun turret onto that car and it could have been retrofitted as a tank. I could have ridden outside on the hood like Slim Pickens in Dr. Strangelove, straddling that bomb to earth like a wild mustang. We never got to see him blown to smithereens at the end of his ride, though.

Most of the time, I couldn't see over the dashboard in that car, but Mom would describe to me all that she could see that she thought I'd like to know about, like her favorite restaurants and which aunt or cousin lived where.

Just as my mom said, Elvis Presley used to drive by my grandmother's house in his green pickup truck with his guitar next to him on the seat, the hip of the guitar nudged up against his own. One day after seeing him drive by and him waving back to us, I excitedly turned on the cement porch and tripped over the glass milk bottles set out for the next morning's exchange. One of the rectangular bottles broke as I fell on it, landing on my knees, skewered by the large shards.

I screamed and screamed from the pain and the fear of the blood as my mother rushed me into the bathroom and set me on her knee to mop up around the lacerations. She pulled one large, angled and glinting piece of glass from under the skin. She worked hard on stopping the flow, her furrowed brow and determination not enough until she gave in and carried my growing but still pudgy body back out into the DeSoto and onto the long vinyl bench seat, my knees each wrapped in large striped towels with the blood already beginning to spot the stripes.

The DeSoto revved up and Mom backed out of the driveway, spinning dirt before jabbing the Drive button on the dashboard and heading down the street the same way Elvis had gone. My mother's attempts at soothing my sobs and screams were spoiled by the look on her face as the car hurtled down the single-story street, the beautiful sunset giving her face a fire-angry countenance. I was not consoled. Mother glanced desperately around the interior of the car for something to distract me and found my brother's toy Rifleman Winchester on the back seat. One hand on the wheel and her leg stretched out to keep her foot jammed on the accelerator, she arched backward over the seat and snatched it up.

"Here, shoot any coloreds you see!", she commanded me. The task of holding my brother's coveted toy gun while trying to comprehend the order to aim it at a people with whom I did not have any reason to dislike did the trick of distracting me from my terrors for the moment.

And in that moment, there was Elvis, returning back down the street in the opposite direction. My mother, despite the urgency of my crisis, actually slowed down as she approached the King's truck.

Elvis slowed down, too. The two vehicles stopped abreast of each other and my mother just smiled, albeit somewhat maniacally. Elvis looked at her, then to me, the rifle on my lap above my wrapped, bloodied knees.

"Ever'thang alright, Ma'am?"

My mother glanced at me dreamily and back to Elvis and slowly nodded, speechless. I protectively raised the rifle to sight down the barrel at Elvis and he brought his right hand to the window sill as a pistol, cocked it, and fired a winking smile at me. I lowered my weapon and smiled back at him.

Elvis put the truck into gear, nodded at my mother and drove on, turning around to follow us out of the neighborhood as I craned my neck to look back over the seat all the way until he turned off to go in another direction.

My mother looked at me, smiled, and jumped on the gas pedal, catapulting us toward the Methodist Hospital emergency room.

~~~

Nowadays, when I am riding shotgun with my mother behind the wheel rocketing down the humidity-soaked, one-hundred-foot-high oak-lined boulevards of Memphis, I remember how Elvis came back to make sure I was alright, because of my mother.

SHE LOVES ME

She Loves me. The scent of the sweetest Narcissus carries her words. When I walk with her, they grow in her footsteps and her child picks them to bring to her in the morning. Together they climb the wooden ladder into her big bed made of down and cumulus and gardenia. The little girl giggles and cries and she gathers the girl in with arms that would be too small to carry a goose from out of the garden but somehow manage to encircle the young one's entire world of concerns and happiness.

She Loves me. And she says that I am Magical for how I conjure the visions of our life together. The places that I take her and show her out in the Universe while holding her hands are new to her and yet are exactly what she has been waiting for, she says. With a rhyme of words, I cast a spell on her that turns her outward toward Heaven and the Angels assist, gifting her with those things that I cannot. With my touch, a fine mist envelops her and dispels all traces of the Other's touch. With a deep, guttural tone I take her inward toward her feminine divinity as she writhes and calls out to Athena and Venus and all of her other Sisters. I forge huge mechanical beasts, the fire fanned by her breath, and when they are complete I cause them to come alive by the Grace of God – for their purpose is to serve her and those she cares for.

She Loves me. And if I am Magic then she is Alchemy. With skill and intellect and care she creates a world around her that is Sufficiency. And more. She manifests the necessities of her life and the lives around her as coal is shaped into diamonds. She manifests in the time span of a moment.

She Loves me. But not as a New Love. Rather, as a burnished love – a well-worn flannel of faded color. Just not new or shiny or untested and tried. She is the well-worn trail smelling of pine sap and fern and dogwood that is sure to lead homeward; the Oriole that is settled in its end-of-season nest lined with everything found for the comfort of its young and its mate.

She Loves me. But the fit. The fit is almost everything. The fit the fit the fit. Is Perfect. The cupping of my body 'round hers is that of the meat of a pecan nested in its shell. The shell rules the shape of the meat. The shapes are married. Our shapes. If it is true that a love is fashioned in Heaven, then how we fit is as the moon fits into its orbit around Mother Earth, and the stars are but the leavings of our dance ended in embrace.

ABOUT THE AUTHOR

Daniel Klein grew up in Pewaukee, Wisconsin — where the circus came to town and for which he worked for a short time. His writing was influenced greatly by the time he spent in Graduate Fiction at the University of Iowa Writer's Workshop.

Daniel is also an accomplished and award-winning artist, photographer, designer, musician, multimedia director, innovator, inventor, actor, director, and consultant. He's been known to fix a kitchen sink or two. His voiceover for Kellogg's Cereals has had over 12 million views on YouTube.

His first novel, LOST IN LOS ALAMOS is searching for a publisher! Daniel now lives with his wife between Thailand and Los Angeles and his desire in life is to be in the enviable position to write about life so that, ultimately, we experience the divine grace of God that's in us and all around us.

Any and all comments are appreciated. Ways to contribute:

> Read: https://coffeehouseblog.com
>
> E-mail: daniel@lightinteractivemedia.com
>
> View: https://instagram.com/iphoneimagescom
>
> Listen: https://kleinvoices.com

If you would like a copy of Pool of Souls and Other Stories or would like to find out about ongoing projects including screenplays, treatments, novels, and inventions, please call, write, or e-mail! Thanks!

www.ingramcontent.com/pod-product-compliance
Lightning Source LLC
Chambersburg PA
CBHW051945170626
46808CB00007B/2486